INSTRUCTIONS FOR HOW TO

MURDER
YOUR WIFE
and
OTHER PEOPLE

—A Horror Novel

H. L. Osterman

ABSOLUTELY AMAZING eBOOKS

Habent Sua Fata Libelli

ABSOLUTELY AMAZING eBOOKS

Manhanset House
Shelter Island Hts., New York 11965-0342

bricktower@aol.com • publisher@absolutelyamazingebooks.com
• absolutelyamazingebooks.com

Library of Congress Cataloging-in-Publication Data
H.L. Osterman
Instructions For How To Murder
Your Wife and Other People—A Horror Novel
p. cm.

1. FICTION / Humorous / Black Humor. 2. FICTION / Horror.
3. FICTION / Ghost. 4. FICTION / Thrillers / Suspense.
Fiction, I. Title.

ISBN: 978-1-955036-69-6, Trade Paper

INSTRUCTIONS
FOR
HOW TO
MURDER
YOUR WIFE
and
OTHER PEOPLE

—A Horror Novel

H. L. Osterman

Other books by H. L. Osterman

Robots and Rust Buckets

Short Changed

Walter the Weirdo

Time Travel and Other Sciene Fiction Journeys

Zane Grey's Illustrated Two-Gun Tales

"Everybody is going to be dead one day, just give them time."

—Neil Gaiman, author of fantasy
and horror novels and comic books.

INTRODUCTION

This book might be called a psychological thriller. Or a horror story. Or a fantasy. Take your pick.

But to be clear, *Instructions for How to Murder Your Wife and Other People* is <u>not</u> a self-help manual or a Do It Yourself book, so take it for what it is: Entertainment.

While I normally spend my time putting together anthologies or writing my *Walter the Weirdo* mystery series, I sometimes turn to darker topics like in my previous novel, *Short Changed*.

Think of this as a companion volume to that latter effort.

According to August House, "Scary stories can show children that it is okay to be afraid and that they can use their brains to solve problems, even when they are frightened or use their natural survival instincts to safely escape from dangerous situations."

That applies to adults too.

Horror Tree says that "cathartic release, often achieved through this process of confronting and realizing important fears and emotions, is natural to the function of the human psyche."

Shaina Weatherhead of Collider explains that horror can "serve as a distraction if we're in a time of intense stress ... Your parasympathetic nervous system works to relax your body after the danger has passed."

The Washington Post takes the discussion one step further: "So why do we like it? It is a combination of an adrenaline rush and an opportunity to learn about dealing with scary situations in a safe environment ..." Researchers, we're told, have identified three main types of horror fans: "adrenaline junkies," "white knucklers" and "dark copers."

Michelle Park of Long Island University says the purpose of horror is "to highlight unconscious fears, desire, urges, and primeval archetypes that are buried deep in our collective subconscious ...." She adds, "It is ironic how we hate the feeling of being scared, but we still enjoy the thrill."

Kim Wong-Shing of CNET sums it up by saying, "Horror can help provide relief from pent-up tension. It's a way to practice feeling scared in a safe environment, refocus your brain away from real-life anxieties, and enjoy the release that comes after the movie is over" ... or the book is ended. She calls it "making friends with fear."

Me, I just call it fun.

-H.L. Osterman

CHAPTER 1

The bomb should have killed me when it blew up. The metal suit protected me except for one dent in the helmet. That indention caused a concussion, cracking my skull like an eggshell. I remained in a coma for seven months.

When I regained consciousness, my wife was standing by the hospital bed. "Are you all right?" I asked her before she could ask me.

"Of course," she replied. "Why wouldn't I be?"

"You were standing next to me when the bomb went off."

"Oh, you and your inventions. You almost killed yourself. I was in the kitchen at the time. It was quite an explosion. Insurance paid for a new living room."

"That's good," I said. But I was puzzled. Before I had lapsed into the coma, I thought I'd seen a bundle of bloody clothes and goo next to me on the floor. Who could that have been?

"How are the kids?" I asked. Worried about those raw red remains.

"John, we have no children. The doctors said that concussion might leave you slightly confused."

"But Randy and Mitzi –?"

"You're thinking of my cousins. Randy and Mitzie came by to visit you, but you were still in dreamland. They said to give you their best when you came out of the coma."

"Uh, yeah. Nice of them."

"Frederick may come by to see you today. He has some papers for you to sign."

"Frederick – who's that?"

"Your business partner, of course. After the explosion, your company lost several major contracts. Concern over safety issues, they claimed. The bomb scared them. Frederick had to sell off a couple of patents. I suspect that's what the papers are about."

"Patents?"

"Yes, dear. But don't worry, you have lots of them."

"Why would I have patents??

"Because you're an inventor, dear. Oh my, I better talk with the doctor. Your memories are more scrambled than I expected."

"Oh, yeah. You just said something about inventions."

"Don't you remember, you were testing your Iron Man suit when you set the bomb off. I wish you hadn't done that in the living room."

"Iron Man – like in the comic book?"

"That's just what you called the suit. It was supposed to be for police bomb squads. It must have worked. You're still alive."

And so are you, I thought to myself.

CHAPTER 2

A man who identified himself as Frederick Woolworth came by to see me. I was sure I'd never laid eyes on him before. He said he was my business partner and I went along with the charade. I was curious what my wife might have put him up to.

He wanted me to sign several papers relating to the sale of patents. One was for a gizmo that created health bars out of phytoplankton. Something about straining sea water. Did I invent that? Oh well, if whales can eat plankton, I suppose people can too.

After I signed the papers, this Woolworth guy shook my hand and said he looked forward to seeing me back at the office. I didn't ask him where the office was. I figured I could look up the address. Maybe I'd remember the company's name in the meantime.

Then the doctor came in and asked me a series of cognitive questions.

"What day is it?"

"Beats me," I said. "I've been in a coma, I'm told. How long – seven months?"

"Do you know the name of the President?"

"President of what – the local Lion's Club? The Ford Motor Company? The NRA?"

"How about the President of the United States?"

I got that one right. There hadn't been a change-over during the time I'd been out like a light.

He held up three fingers. "How many?" he said.

I got that one right too.

"Do you have any depressing thoughts?" he wanted to know.

"No," I answered. I didn't mention that I was bummed the bomb idea hadn't worked.

"Do you have any suicidal feelings?"

"No," I replied.

"You're over them?"

"I didn't have any. I wasn't trying to commit suicide with that bomb. That's why I was wearing the metal suit."

"Where did you get that suit of armor?"

"I invented it. Apparently, that is what I do."

"You seem to have partial memory," concluded the doctor. "But it may take a while for all your memory to come back."

"I'll wait," I said. "When can I go home?"

~ ~ ~

When I walked through the front door, I was greeted by thundering feet, a lolling tongue, and wagging tail. "Rex, did you miss me?" I said to the excited Golden Retriever.

The dog would have knocked me over if my wife hadn't been there steadying me with her hand on my arm. "Down, boy," she said. Rex immediately sat, showing his obedience. She must have sent him to a trainer while I was in the hospital. I didn't remember him being so compliant.

I reached down to stroke his ears. He seemed to like that. "Good Rex," I said. He'd always been a man's dog.

That's why I was surprised when he moved over to stand beside my wife, looking up adoringly at her. That was insult to injury. While I was hovering near death in a coma, she had stolen my pooch.

CHAPTER 3

Home from the hospital, I started researching poisons on the Internet. Amazing what you can find. After much consideration, I decided on that old stand-by, arsenic. It has been called the "king of poisons" – and "inheritance powder" due to its historical use in killing off family members. It is quite toxic.

One benefit for me: it had an antidote called succimer. That was good.

Arsenic Powder can be bought online. I won't share the website with you. And succimer is available from your local pharmacy under the brand name Chemet.

That wasn't so hard.

Buying them under phony names was trickier. But if you're clever, it can be done. Trust me on that.

The idea was to put the arsenic in our morning coffee, enough to kill a horse. She wouldn't be suspicious if we both drank the coffee. Then I would take the antidote.

Next thing I knew, I woke up in the hospital. The doctor was standing over me, a stern look on his face. "We need to talk about those suicidal thoughts," he announced, studying his clipboard as if reading from a prepared script.

"I didn't try to commit suicide," I corrected him.

"You had enough arsenic in you to kill you three times over. Lucky you took that succimer at the last minute."

"See?"

"That arsenic didn't get in your coffee by accident."

"I was testing a new invention." It was a lie, but I couldn't admit I was trying to murder my wife. People get upset over things like that.

"An invention? What would that be?"

"Uh, using arsenic as a cure for cancer." Okay, it was the best I could do on short notice.

"You don't have cancer."

"I was in the placebo control group."

"Ohmygod, you haven't given arsenic to others, have you?"

"No, I was just starting the test phase," I backtracked quickly.

"Thank goodness for that. But we're going to have to report this incident to the police."

"Wish you wouldn't do that. It was just an experiment. I promise to give up on that project and go to the next one on my list."

"What would that be?"

"Turning lead into gold."

"Isn't that alchemy?"

"Only until it works."

"Sorry, but we still have to file a report. I expect somebody will come by to talk with you."

"Okay, if those are the rules."

"In the meantime, we will continue to detox you. We were able to administer chelating agents administered within hours of the arsenic absorption. Gut decontamination and hemodynamic stabilization are key factors in the initial management of acute arsenic intoxication. We undertook gastric lavage to prevent further absorption. I see no signs of renal failure, so we can dispense with hemodialysis. Recovery may take months, but we will watch your progress closely."

"Thanks, Doc."

"Just doing our job. But we've got to get you in a better state of mind. Get rid of those suicidal tendencies."

"By the way, how's my wife."

"Your wife?"

"Same last name as mine. Check your patient list."

"There's no other patient by that name in this hospital."

~ ~ ~

My wife came by to visit later that afternoon. She looked great, her auburn hair spilling onto her shoulders. She wore a beaded mesh blouson dress by Adrianna Papell. Her eyes sparkled like green peridots. She had a spring in her step.

I didn't dare ask how she escaped that dose of arsenic in her coffee. Did she somehow feint drinking it? Was she onto my scheme?

"Hi, dear," she said. "How are you feeling?"

"Like I've got a bulldozer in my gut."

"That will pass, the doctor says."

"How are you?"

"Same as always."

"That's good," I lied.

"How did you get that arsenic? We don't have anything like that around the house. Not even rat poison or pesticides."

"I was working on another invention. Guess it didn't pan out."

"I should say not. You've got to tackle less dangerous projects. First, the bomb; now, this arsenic."

"Makes me think of that old movie – *Arsenic and Old Lace*. That one with Cary Grant who has two doddery old aunts who are poisoning people by putting arsenic in elderberry tea."

"They say you took your arsenic in a cup of coffee."

"Yes, that seemed a good way to ingest it for my experiment."

"Lucky I didn't drink any of it by mistake."

"Yes, lucky," I said. But that left me puzzled. I'd put the coffee in the pot myself, added the arsenic powder, poured the coffee into her cup, handed it to her at the breakfast table, watched her sip it.

What went wrong?

CHAPTER 4

Maybe a car wreck, I told myself. I had been home from the hospital for a week now and had had time to think about it. Our old clunker – a 2004 Ford Taurus – had many things that could go wrong with it. Faulty brakes. A blown-out tire. A fire in the engine. Hit by a truck. You name it.

The trick would be fooling the insurance company.

My other policy – United Heath – was giving me a hard time, not wanting to cover the hospital expenses for the arsenic. Calling it attempted suicide. I stuck with the claim of accidental poisoning.

The police wanted to know where the "accidental" poison came from. I repeated the experiment story and gave them the receipts for my purchases. "I'm an inventor," I said. Remembering my failed bomb experiment, they chuckled and suggested I should consider changing professions.

My so-called partner Frederick Woolworth greeted me warmly when I showed up at Wonder Works Inc. My wife had reminded me of the address. I was surprised that the company had two other employees – a receptionist and a lab assistant.

Posters on the wall extolled some of the company's inventions. Had I been the one who came up with the automatic toilet paper dispenser?

"While you've been gone, we've continued plowing ahead," said Woolworth. "Most of our attention has been on the solar-power lawnmower. The application for a patent has been filed. We have three major companies who want to license the technology. That was a great concept you had. Randy here took your plans and tinkered with them and – *voilà* – it worked!"

My plans? A lawnmower? Maybe it was part of my lingering amnesia. The concussion had left blank spaces in my memory. Best I could recall, I never mowed the lawn. At home, we had a yard service – a truckload of Mexicans who miraculously appeared once a month and *zip*! *zip*! mowed the lawn, trimmed the hedges, watered the flowers, and cleaned the gutters in about 20 minutes time. Why would I be thinking about a solar-powered lawnmower?

"Good job," I said, patting Randy on the shoulder. He was a chubby man with thinning blond hair. He wore a white lab coat. Round Harry Potter glasses covered his eyes.

"Thanks," Randy beamed, his smile as wide as a four-lane highway. He seemed to value my opinion.

I figured if I could invent a solar-powered lawnmower, I could figure out how to make our ancient Ford Taurus into a deathtrap. Just needed to get the old noodle going. No doubt I'd think of something.

"Mitzi's been a big help while you were gone," added Woolworth. "She's taken over some of the bookkeeping."

"Mitzi –?"

"She's been a lifesaver," he nodded toward the young brunette at the reception desk. The woman wore a tight pink sweater and a short blue skirt. She didn't look very busy.

Randy and Mitzi – I'd thought those were my kids' names. That was when I was first coming out of the coma. But my wife had explained we had no children, that Randy and Mitzi were her cousins.

"Are you my wife's cousin?" I asked. Confused.

"Who?"

"My wife, are you related to her?"

"No, of course not."

Now Mitzi had my curiosity working overtime. "Are you and our lab assistant married?"

"Oh, you're such a tease, always claiming I have a crush on Randy. But you know I'm engaged and that Randy is gay."

"John, maybe it's too soon for you to come back to work," said Woolworth, taking my arm and gently steering me toward the door.

"No, I'm fine."

"But all this crazy talk about 'your wife's cousins' shows you're still on the mend. The doctors said your memory might be scrambled for a while, but it would gradually restore itself. You just need more time."

"Ignore me. Like you say, it will all come back."

~ ~ ~

Sitting at the drawing board in my small office at Wonder Works, I tried to come up with some new ideas. After all, I was an inventor. Ideas R Us, as we used to joke around the office. Wasn't I the guy who came up with the self-buttering toaster? At least, one of the posters on the reception area wall said so.

That made me wonder why we had a reception area. Wasn't like this was a business that had any visitors. Nobody dropped by to buy new ideas. Nobody called on us. We offered no services to the public. What did Mitzi do – other than some of the bookkeeping now?

No ideas popped into my head. I was drawing a blank. Maybe if I focused on one topic. Say, the home. Better still, the kitchen. What was needed in the kitchen? No clue, I admitted to myself. At home, Mrs. Mueller did all the cooking.

This was not going well, but Frederick Woolworth didn't seem to notice. Best I could figure out, ol' Fred filed the patents and did the licensing – sort of a glorified salesman. Me, I was the idea man, the one who figured out how to make some gizmo work. Randy was my assistant, helping construct whatever device it was. Mitzi, I had no idea what she did.

Despite her denial, I wondered if Mitzi was actually my wife's cousin. It wasn't a common name. Other than my daughter, the only person I'd ever heard of with that name was Mitzi Gaynor, the actress who starred in *South Pacific*. The one who was gonna wash that man right outta her hair.

Now I had Mitzis and Randys coming out of the woodwork. Was I getting them confused in my topsy-turvy mental state?

When I got home, I would ask my wife about Mitzi again. Maybe I was just confused about her cousin.

By the end of the day, I had come up with a short list – all bad ideas.

> A drone that automatically polices the parameters of your property.
> A popsicle that contains your daily vitamins.
> A parking meter that issues tickets for expired parking.
> A bicycle bell that rings whenever someone steps in front of your bike.
> A camera-doorbell that automatically snaps a digital photo of your visitors.
> A laser knife for cutting cheese.

I didn't even bother showing the list to Woolworth.

CHAPTER 5

The next day was Saturday. My wife had gone over to Klett's Bookstore, a ramshackle emporium of both new and used books out on Highway 102. She had said she was looking for a book on memory loss and amnesia. I think she fancied herself a latter-day Clara Barton, determined to cure my lingering afflictions on her own.

To my chagrin, I had not made any progress on how to make our car explode in a fiery inferno. That was frustrating, for I was supposed to be an inventive genius.

However, I had come up with an alternate plan. If I could get her in the car, I could drive it off that cliff at Deadman's Bend. Me, I could jump out at the last minute. Let her take the fall. Nobody had ever survived going over that vertical 80-foot drop. Sharp rocks at the bottom were like mineralized punji stakes.

I fed Rex a dish of Alpo as I thought more about it. This was a good plan, I told myself. Other cars had gone over that cliff, hence the creepy name for that stretch of road. One more wouldn't be suspicious.

If I was going to do something, now was as good a time as any.

Klett's was just outside the town limit. Getting there would be a bit of a hike, but she had the car, so I decided to hoof it before the day got any hotter. The temperature was in the 90s. Our town being in a valley, I had to make my way up a steep section of 102, crossing the hump of Mesa Linda before coming to the bookstore.

Not in great shape, I was winded by the time I reached the edge-of-town store. Before I started down the driveway, I stopped to catch my breath and survey the scene. The three-story building looked like the House of the Seven Gables gone to seed. The unpainted clapboard siding was weathered with age. The building would have qualified as a Historic Site if anything important had ever happened here or if Nathaniel Hawthorne had bothered to write a novel about it.

Parked in front of the building was my Ford Taurus along with two or three other cars, customers no doubt. And off to the far side of the building was the retired orange school bus that Marlon Klett had bought on a whim. Klett was a wannabe hippie, dreaming of outfitting the interior of the bus and heading out on a road trip. He wanted to see the Grand Canyon, he told his customers when rhapsodizing about his forthcoming Golden Years. In his early 60s, Klett was approaching retirement age.

Inside the bookstore the air was musty with the smell of books, magazines, and old newspapers. Estelle Bennington (Marlon's common law wife) was at the cash register. An overhead sign shaped like an arrow said PAY HERE. A couple of customers were milling about, squinting at book titles and thumbing through magazines displayed on wire racks.

I didn't see my wife here in the main room, but the bookstore was like a rabbit warren, a series of interconnected rooms in what had once been a large boarding house. The History Section in one room, Science Fiction in another, Mystery in still another. Even a Children's Book Nook upstairs.

The shop had several amenities. There was a free-to-customers Reference Room where the thick volumes were not for sale. Also, a Book Exchange where people could trade in hardbacks they had finished reading. In the corner was a large silver coffee urn, offering a cup of Maxwell House for a 25¢ donation. Dozens of glazed donuts rested under a handwritten sign that said Take One.

While waiting for my wife to turn up, I asked Estelle if I could use the Reference Room's Book Index. She led me into a side room where trays of index cards listed all the volumes in the free section. "Here you go, help yourself," she smiled.

I thumbed through the cards looking for books on how to murder someone and get away with it. Nowhere did I find that exact topic, but there were a couple of interesting choices. Following the numbers inked on the 4x6 cards, I traced my way down the lines of books on the surrounding shelves, plucking out one here, another there.

This research was merely backup in case my car-off-the-cliff plan went astray. After all, I hadn't been very successful so far – the bomb hadn't worked, the poison hadn't worked. I blamed my ineptitude on the after effects of my concussion. It had left me confused. Sometimes my head hurt, like a tiny blacksmith pounding on an anvil inside my cranium. But that was not going to deter me from my avowed mission of murdering my wife. She was as good as dead.

One book titled *Fun with Electricity* gave me some new ideas. Another called *Legal Challenges to Slip-and-Fall Insurance Claims* offered more suggestions. And *Poisonous Mushrooms to Avoid* provided food for thought. When you think about it, there are lots of ways to die.

Did you know hippos kill 26,000 people each year in Africa? That autoerotic asphyxiation takes out 600 adventurous lovers annually? Icicles kill 400 a year in Russia? Some 450 people die from falling out of bed? Ants kill 30 people per year? Vending machine kill 13 people every year?

How does a vending machine kill you? Apparently, by toppling over and crushing you. So much for kicking the machine when it steals your change without delivering a soda. I didn't trust machines, even though I sometimes invented them.

411 people are electrocuted each year. These are mainly workers, not stupid children who stick a fork in an electrical outlet or those who drop a hairdryer in the bathtub. Counting them would make the casualties much higher.

Did you know one home fire-related death occurs every three hours and eight minutes? Or that each year, more than 400 Americans die from unintentional carbon monoxide poisoning, mainly from unvented space heaters in the home.

Another 2,000 commit suicide by carbon monoxide, usually in a motor vehicle.

"Suicide" by a hose in the car's tailpipe – that was a workable scenario. And a hairdryer in the bathtub might be easy to arrange. Death by ants or hippos would be much harder to manage.

But back to my current plan: Driving the car off the cliff at Deadman's Bend. Where was my wife? Once I found her, I would offer to drive her home, then at the top of the hill make a wrong turn.

I wandered from room to room, looking for her. Finally, I found her in the Children's Book Nook. That was a strange place, considering we had no children. I reminded myself to ask her again about Randy and Mitzi. I would've sworn those were the names of our kids. I didn't remember any of her relatives by those names, particularly favorite cousins who would visit me in the hospital. And what about the names of my employees? Was that merely a coincidence? What are the odds of that, I asked myself? It was all so very confusing.

"Hi dear," I greeted her.

"What are you doing here?" she asked with raised eyebrows. She was actually a very beautiful woman. She had luxurious auburn hair and green eyes. This had once appealed to me, but that time had passed.

"Thought I'd come up here and drive you home."

"You walked all the way?"

"How else could I have got here?"

"A taxi? An Uber? Perhaps Frederick would drop you off?"

"I thought a walk would be good for me," I smiled pleasantly. I had gotten quite good at faking my emotions. "Perhaps on the way home we could stop at the Tastee Treat for a snow cone. It's pretty hot out there."

"How thoughtful."

"I remembered you like their peppermint cones."

"Yes, it reminds me of Christmas."

"The kids always love Christmas."

"What kids, dear? Do you mean Randy and Mitzi's children?"

"Yes," I lied. "That's who I meant."

"We should invite Randy and Mitzi to dinner soon. They have a new babysitter."

"How old are their kids? I forget."

"Of course, you do. You never remember their birthdays."

"Time slips by so fast," I equivocated.

"Doesn't it. I'm ready to go if you are."

"Sure. Any books to pay for?"

"No, I spent most of my time in the Medical and Health Room. I gleaned some good advice on how to help you restore your memory."

"I remember most things," I insisted stubbornly.

"Oh? What are the names of Randy and Mitzi's children."

"I don't even remember Randy and Mitzi," I admitted.

~ ~ ~

"I'll drive," I volunteered. That wasn't suspicious. I usually drove when the two of us went out. Yes, I remembered that much.

"Sure," she smiled, handing me the car keys.

Inserting the key in the ignition, I gave it a turn.

Bzzz-zzzz.

The engine turned over, but didn't start. I tried again.

Bzzz-zzzz-zzz.

Nothing.

"Shall I call Triple A?" she asked, holding up her iPhone.

"Give me a sec here." I tried again.

Bzzz-zzzz.

The car was necessary to my plan. Deadman's Bend awaited.

Bzzz-zzzz-zzz.

"Well, that sucks," I said.

My wife was on the phone. "Triple A can have someone here in a half hour," she reported. "That Texaco on 102 is an affiliate. They're pretty close."

"No, I'm sure the car will start if we let it sit for a while. Let the battery regain its charge."

"But I need to get home. I have a cake to bake."

"You don't cook. Mrs. Mueller comes over five days a week to make our dinners."

She smiled at me sadly. "Dear, you know I'm famous for my strawberry upside-down shortcake. It won first place at the Community Center's Bake Off."

"It did?"

"And you love my Lobster Risotto. And my Butter-Basted Sous Vide Pork Chops with Fennel and Coriander."

"You can make that?"

"Quit teasing me. You know those are my strong points in the kitchen."

"Then what does Mrs. Mueller do?"

"She does the housekeeping. You know, vacuums the floors, changes the sheets, does the laundry. She's a treasure. I don't know what I'd do without here."

"Are you sure she doesn't do the cooking?"

"Dear, I was planning on making pork chops for dinner tonight."

"Guess we'd better get you home then," I said, eager to get to Deadman's Bend.

"How, dear? The battery's dead."

"I have an idea."

CHAPTER 6

"Hey, Marlon, got a favor to ask."

"Sure. Take any book in the store. You can pay me later. By the way, you have my and Estelle profound sympathy."

"For what?"

"That bomb. A shame what happened." He let his voice trail off. His face taking on a somber look.

"Oh that. I'm doing well. My metal suit protected me except for a bump on the head. I'm fine."

"Yes, I can see that." He sounded like he was accusing me of something, some heinous act that he refused to say out loud. Underneath his sympathetic words I could detect some kind of attitude that I didn't like. Well, to hell with Marlon Klett. He was an old fool who would never see the Grand Canyon. He'd drop dead behind his cash register, that was for sure.

Sighing, I got straight to the point. "My car battery is dead. Can I borrow your bus? Promise I'll return it tomorrow morning."

"I don't mind. But its battery is probably dead too. I haven't driven it since the Fourth of July parade last month."

"Let me give it a try."

Klett reached into a drawer below his cash register. "Here you go, the keys. But don't say I didn't warn you."

~ ~ ~

"Over here," I beckoned to my wife. "We're borrowing Marlon's bus."

"Really, dear. I'd feel like I was riding home in a clown car."

Turning the key, I listened to the orange bus groan, shutter, then kick into life.

Zzzz-sptt-zzz. Bazzzzz!

"Hurry up," I shouted. "I don't know how long this rattletrap will keep running."

"Oh, very well." She locked the Taurus and sauntered over the bus, looking at it like it was a death trap. Little did she know.

"Triple A will have a fit," she predicted. "Coming out, but us not being here."

"Let them complain," I called from the school bus. "We'll just say they took too long."

"If that's what you want."

"Watch your step," I said as she climbed onto the bus. She had to hike up her skirt to reach the first step. I wondered how small school children managed to get up those steep steps every day.

"Oh, damn, I broke one of my heels," she complained.

"You're wearing flats," I said.

"I mean I got a run in my hose."

"You're not wearing hosiery, for God's sake. Get in the bus and take a seat." I felt like I was speaking to an unruly child. Randy was like that, I told myself. But wait – that must be some kind of false memory. Wasn't Randy the guy who worked for me at Wonder Works?

"Satisfied?" she grumbled, plopping down in the worn-slick seat behind the driver.

Today, *I* was the driver. Letting out the clutch, the big orange monolith lurched forward and lumbered up the driveway toward highway. Traffic was light on 102 at this time of day, allowing the bus to crawl along at 30 MPH, not having to match the speed of fast-moving vehicles. The bus must've had a governor that limited its top speed. Pedal to the metal only got it up to 45. I hoped that would be enough torque to break through the metal guardrail at Deadman's Bend.

The town was in the valley. The road down to it was steep enough that there were runoffs for trucks whose brakes gave out. I wondered if the bus had good brakes? It was old and rattly, built in the early '80s. But no need to find out; we weren't going that far.

Deadman's Bend was a curve in the road that signaled the upcoming descent into the valley. There was a large oak on one side, a tree that never seemed to have any leaves. On the other was a low railing between the road and a precipice that dropped straight down to craggy rocks. Some 38 cars had gone over during the last dozen years, none of the passengers surviving. This stretch of highway had earned its dramatic name with its death toll.

As I approached the curve, I kept the steering wheel straight, aiming for the railing. Pulling a lever, I tried to make the hinged doors swing outward from the hull of the bus. But the doors remained stuck shut. I didn't have time to stop the bus. Yanking on the lever again, they parted a foot or so, enough to squeeze through. At the last second, I leapt out, landing hard on the pavement. I think I dislocated my shoulder. It really hurt.

I heard a crash, metal against metal, as the big school bus broke through the barrier, plunging over the side of the cliff. Like counting for lightning after hearing thunder – *one Mississippi, two Mississippi* – I got to *four Mississippi's* before I heard it hit the rocks below.

Ka-blamm!

Struggling to my feet, I stretched my shoulder until it gave a *pop!* – then moved over to the broken guard rail to peer over the edge. My movements were tentative because I have a fear of heights. Squinting my eyes, I could see the ruined bus at the bottom of the gorge. It looked like a wadded-up piece of orange construction paper, tossed away by some petulant child.

Didn't my daughter Mitzi once throw a tantrum over a drawing that didn't turn out right, crumpling the paper and throwing it into the waste basket beside her desk? No, that couldn't be right. Mitzi was the receptionist at my office. Why was I getting that confused?

Turning away from the cliff, I sat under the skeletal oak tree to wait for the next motorist to come along. Let them call 9-1-1. I hadn't brought my cell phone. A new Apple iPhone 14, I hadn't wanted to risk damaging it when I jumped out of the moving vehicle. You have to think ahead.

~ ~ ~

After the paramedics checked me out and I gave the police my story about faulty brakes, a nice sergeant drove me home. I didn't know him, but he was very solicitous. He said they would inform me about the condition of my wife after the rescue squad got to the bottom of the gorge. It would take a crane with a long wire rope to pull the wreckage out. But first, that same crane, with a bucket attached to its sheave, would lower the rescuers one-by-one to the bottom. Nobody expected to encounter a survivor.

But when I walked into the house, I was greeted by a cheery, "Hi dear, what took you so long to get home?"

I stood there, my mouth open, gasping like a fish just pulled up from its watery environment. "H-how ... how ...?" I sputtered, staring at my wife. She had changed from slacks to a billowy Fensace sundress with a floral design. She was clearly unscathed, no scratches or contusions. Not a single auburn hair on her head was out of place.

"It was so nice of Mr. Klett to give me a ride home. I had no intention of going on that horrid bus."

"But you –" I couldn't speak.

She glanced out the picture window. "Where is that dilapidated old school bus? We can't have one parked in the driveway. The neighbors will complain. They might think you've taken a part-time job ferrying children to and from Morningside Elementary. We can't have that."

"The bus had a wreck," I finally got the words out. "It went over the cliff at Deadman's Bend. I thought you were in it."

"My goodness! Are you all right?" she exclaimed, noticing my torn clothes for the first time.

"I barely escaped with my life," I gave a sob. "The brakes were bad on that old bus."

"Thank goodness, you're safe," said my wife, hugging me. She felt cold against my skin. I hoped I wasn't going into shock. I had taken quite a tumble coming out of that bus. Maybe I'd hit my head again, another concussion. But later, probing around my scalp, running my fingers through my hair, everything felt normal.

CHAPTER 7

I paid Marlon Klett $700 for the loss of his school bus. I heard he'd bought it for only $300 at an automobile auction. But I wasn't going to quibble.

After accepting the money, the bastard banned me from the bookstore for life. Punishment for destroying his bus. I was pissed by his pettiness. I'd never really liked him.

On the other hand, my wife adored Marlon and Estelle. They used to treat her like a guest of honor at the bookstore. Now, I was *persona non grata* on his computerized customer list. It wasn't fair.

At work, Frederick Woolworth and Randy – I'd learned his last name was Gibson – were finalizing a production model of one of my earlier inventions, a light bulb that turned on when you walked into a room. No it didn't plug into a sensor; the bulb itself was sensitive to movement. I don't remember designing the thing.

There had been problems with the movement-detecting light bulb. For those people who tossed and turned in their sleep, the light would be flashing off and on all night long. The solution was simple: simply switch off the light when you go to bed. "Simplicity is the ultimate sophistication," as Leonardo da Vinci said.

I still had trouble believing Randy was gay. He had no outward signs, like swishiness or a lisp. And he seemed all too familiar with Mitzi to be a homosexual. They always left work together. When I asked about it, she merely said, "Ride sharing."

Mitzi herself was another question. One day I asked Woolworth what she did. "Everything," he replied.

As for me, I knew that I wasn't earning my keep. I'd had no workable ideas in months. My partner was decent about it, never pushing me to produce. The closest I came was an idea for a self-vacuuming vacuum machine, but Frederick reminded me the Roomba had been out for years. Oh well, that just showed it was a good idea.

Maybe I should buy a Roomba for Mrs. Mueller, I told myself. Make her housekeeping duties a little lighter. I wasn't sure why, but I often saw her in the kitchen, cooking. Her Butter-Basted Sous Vide Pork Chops with Fennel and Coriander was delicious.

One morning as I was leaving for work, I called out to my wife, "See you later, hon. I'll be home by six." I gave Rex a pat on the head and picked up my leather Maxwell Scott briefcase. I don't know why I bothered to carry a briefcase. There were no brilliant ideas for inventions stored in its depths.

"Wait," came my wife's voice. "Don't forget the children. It's your day to drop them off at school."

"Children?"

On cue, a curly-haired little girl walked into the room, a bookbag on her shoulders. "Good morning, daddy," she beamed.

"A-are you Mitzi?" I asked cautiously. She appeared to be about seven or eight. Blonde tresses surrounded her face like a bonnet. I was sure I'd never seen her before.

"Of course, silly daddy. You're teasing me again."

"Let's go," I said, reaching for the door again. "I'll get you to school."

"Don't leave Randy,"

"Who?"

"My slow-poke brother. He's still getting dressed."

Before I could respond, a boy of about ten stalked into the room. He had neatly-combed sandy hair and a red bowtie, a little dandy by the looks of him. "Here I am, daddy" he announced. "Couldn't find my history book. Big test today."

Turning to my wife, I asked, "Where do they go to school?"

"Morningside Elementary – you know that. You take them two days a week when I'm tied up with my Happy Housewives Breakfast Club. I have to be there. I'm president this year."

"That you are," I said, even though I don't remember what the Breakfast Club does. Was it a charity organization? Or simply a gabfest for women in the neighborhood.

"Thank you, dear. Drive careful." She was probably referring to my totaling Marlon Klett's school bus.

Pausing at the door, I said, "By the way, how do I get to Morningside Elementary?"

"Same as always. Left out of the driveway to the end of the street. Then left, right, and another left. You'll see it, that two-story red-brick building with a flagpole out front."

"Sure, I remember," I fibbed. "Come along, kids."

~ ~ ~

Along the drive, I tried to strike up a conversation with my young passengers. I wanted to find out who they really were. "You said you have a history quiz today?" I queried the one who called himself Randy."

"No, daddy. I said I have a math quiz today. I hate numbers."

"How about you?" I said to the girl pretending to be my daughter Mitzi. "Any tests today?"

She continued looking out the car window, all but ignoring me. "Not really."

"Where do you live?" I slipped in an unexpected question.

"You know," she replied. "717 Morning Glory Drive."

"No, that's where I live. Where *you* live?"

"Daddy, are you kicking us out of our home?" asked Randy from the backseat. "Mommy won't like that."

"Never mind," I said, turning my attention to the road. "I think I see your school up ahead."

Morningside Elementary was nothing like my wife had described it. No flagpole, just a plastic statue of a fish. I'd later learn that their junior soccer team was known as the Morningside Guppies. Why it had a piscium mascot was anybody's guess. The school was hundreds of miles from the ocean.

And the building was not two-story brick, but one of those labyrinthian one-story structures constructed of wood and windows. But the ant-like presence of children confirmed that it was indeed an elementary school.

I dropped off Randy and Mitzi. "Am I supposed to pick you up?"

"Mommy does that," said Mitzi, looking at me like I was an idiot.

Were these really my kids? Or had my wife hired stand-ins, child actors playing a part? If so, they were darn good.

CHAPTER 8

When I got home that evening, Mrs. Mueller was setting the table. There was a plate for only one. "Where is everybody?" I asked.

She looked up, puzzled. "Everybody?"

"Never mind," I changed the subject. "What's for dinner."

"Your favorite," she replied. "Lobster Risotto."

Her Lobster Risotto was certainly as good as my wife's, although I couldn't remember last time my wife had made it. Lobster was expensive these days, flown in from Maine. Charlie's Quality Charcuterie was known for its imported meat and fish.

When my wife got home around 8 o'clock, I asked where she'd been.

"My bridge club," she replied, giving me a weird look. "I reminded you this morning."

"You did?"

"Yes, you know I play bridge with the girls every Tuesday night."

"Oh, right," I faked it. "By the way, where are the kids? Do they have a sleepover?"

"What kids? Do you mean my cousins' children?"

"Your cousins?" I was caught off guard.

"Randy and Mitzi, they have two kids."

I said, "How could Randy and Mitzi have children? They're still in elementary school."

"My cousins Randy and Mitzi, I mean."

"I'm taking about our children – the ones I took to school this morning."

My wife looked concerned. "Dear, you must be having another one of your spells."

"Spells? I don't have spells."

"The doctor told you on your last visit that these bouts of confusion might linger for a while."

"Don't blame this on that old injury. That was nearly nine months ago. I'm well, I tell you."

"Recovery takes time." She sounded very patient.

"Most concussions clear up within four weeks," I challenged her words. "I looked it up in that book you borrowed from Klett's Bookstore."

"Yes, I know. That's why we're so concerned about you."

"But what about the kids?"

"We have no children, dear, you know that."

"Oh yeah? If we have no children, why do we have a family dog?"

I had her there.

~ ~ ~

I didn't mention the children again that week. And neither did she. It was like they never existed, that I hadn't dropped them off at Morningside Elementary just the other day. That strengthened my suspicion that those two little rug rats had been child actors, hired on the pretext of playing a joke. They certainly had performed well.

Maybe I should have gone to the Morningside administration office and checked on their enrollment, but I suspect it would have been a waste of time. No Randy and Mitzi would've shown up on the school records if they had been phony.

But wait, I told myself, my own children's names would be on the school's books. But wouldn't the teachers recognize the substitution?

All of these thoughts left me confused. I remembered having kids, or thought I did. Just not those two. Which left the question, where had my wife stashed ours? Nine months was a long time for them to be visiting with my wife's cousins. Or to be off to some faraway boarding school. I wondered if I should file a Missing Persons report, but decided it was too risky. The less exposure to the police, the better.

~ ~ ~

My wife had been involved with the local Little Theater, even appeared in a play called *Evening Breeze*. It was a small part. That had been a couple of years ago, best I could remember. Lately, she had spent her energies with playing bridge and being president of the Happy Housewives Breakfast Club.

It occurred to me she might have found some child actors through her connections at the Little Theater. Calling the "barn" where the Little Theater put on its plays, I reached Randall Tidesdale, the creative director. Another Randy?

"Hi John, what can I do for you? Only got a moment. I'm in the middle of putting on a new production of *The Music Man*. You'd be surprised how few trombone players we have in this town."

"Just a quick question," I assured him. "Did my wife recently get some child actors from you, a boy and a girl?"

"Why would she do that?"

"Some promotion she's working on," I tried to be vague.

"No, I haven't talked to your wife in over a year. But pass along the message that she should come in and audition for the part of Marion the Librarian. She would be a shoo-in, I think."

"I'll tell her," I lied.

"Thanks."

"If she didn't get any child actors through you, where would she have found some?"

"Why are you asking?"

"I think we owe them money."

"Oh. In that case, you might try that talent agency over on Crosstown Boulevard. They place actors."

"I'll give them a try. Thanks, Randall."

"I hope everything's all right. I haven't heard from your wife since I got back from my European tour last fall. That's unlike her."

~ ~ ~

Checking the Yellow Pages in the phone book, I found a listing for Silver Screen Talent Agency. The accompanying ad promised:

Management for Upcoming
Actors and Actresses
Our clients are available for
theatrical productions, films, trade
show presentations.
Reasonable rates.
Test with our Talent Scouts.
You may be the next big star!

I dialed the number at the bottom of the ad and a pleasant woman's voice answered. "Silver Screen Talent," she intoned with precise enunciation. "How may we help you?"

"Do you rent out actors?"

"We represent diverse talent that is available for paid assignments."

"What kind of assignments?"

"Independent films, stage productions, personal appearances. That sort of thing. Are you looking for an actor?"

"Maybe. Would you have anyone available for a private joke?

"A joke?"

"Me and the others guys at the office want to play a trick on our boss. We'd need an actor to help us pull it off. Do you do that sort of thing?"

"Not normally, but we might be able to assist you. It depends on the nature of this ... joke."

"How about kids? Do you have children – say, seven to ten years old?"

"We have a number of talented youngsters. They are very popular in television ads."

"Have you done this sort of thing lately? Say, two kids seven and ten, hired to play a prank on a local family?"

"I can't say we have, but I'm sure we can accommodate your needs. May I have your name, Mr. –?"

But she didn't get a name. By then I had hung up.

CHAPTER 9

Maybe I'm losing it, but I could have sworn I had two children, a ten-year-old boy named Randolph and a seven-year-old girl named Maria. Randy and Mitzi, for short. But they were nowhere to be seen. The house was empty except for me and the missus and the family dog.

Those two imposters – child actors hired by my wife, I was convinced – had been the right age, but looked nothing like my kids. Mitzi had been a redhead like her mom; Randy had my dimpled chin. These kids had been blonde and bland, like central casting for a remake of *Children of the Damned*.

But that still didn't explain what happened to the originals.

Why would my wife hide them away? Why would she try to pass off a couple of young shams as our children? What was her game here?

Could I be sure about having two kids? I didn't know. My mind had been playing tricks on me lately. Well, ever since coming out of the coma. Had that concussion scrambled my brain? Was my mind being bombarded with false memories? Had I lost my tenuous grip on sanity? It was beginning to feel like it.

Taking a deep breath, I sat back in my La-Z-Boy recliner and thought about it. Was I going crazy? I was no longer sure what was real and what wasn't.

Perhaps I should try this from another angle, I told myself.

After the bomb went off, I remembered – or thought I remembered – seeing a pile of bloody rags that I'd thought was my wife's dead body. But that couldn't be right, for she was right here, going about her day-to-day life, attending her Breakfast Club meetings, playing bridge with her friends, as if nothing happened.

If it wasn't my wife who had been killed by the explosion, who could those bloody rags have been?

Then it hit me, as staggering as a sledgehammer to the chest. No, it couldn't be true. But it did make sense – the rags had been Randy and Mitzi.

Ohmygod, had I blown up my children?

That would explain why they were missing.

Had she hired those youthful actors to pose as our children to spare me the trauma of knowing I'd killed Randy and Mitzi with my bomb? That might make sense. She could very well do something like that.

But then again, what had happened to those two sham children? Why had they disappeared too? Had my wife realized she wouldn't be able to pull off the deception, knowing that I had recognized the pair as phonies? Maybe she had canceled the plan as being too unwieldy? Paying the young neophytes their standard day rate and sending them packing?

This hypothesis seemed to fit together like pieces of a jigsaw puzzle.

I felt a wave of grief sweep over me like a tsunami. I couldn't speak. I sat there rocking back and forth in the La-Z-Boy, hugging my knees.

I must have been hunkered there in the overstuffed chair for over an hour or more when a voice inside my head said, Snap out of it. You are grieving over kids who may never have existed. And those two youthful pretenders may simply have been figments of your imagination, the hallucinations of a madman.

I wonder what was wrong with me.

~ ~ ~

My theory did a loop-de-loop when I came down for breakfast the next morning and found two children waiting for me at the dinette table. They looked nothing like the previous counterfeits, these two being dark-haired and as serious a Hitler Youth group.

"Hello, Father," said the girl formally. "Won't you join us for breakfast? We are having cereal this morning."

"Kellogg Fruit Loops," added the boy.

Fruit Loops sounded very appropriate.

"Who are you?" I asked. "Don't say Randy and Mitzi."

"Who else would we be?" replied the ersatz Randy.

"Yes," said the girl. "I am your daughter Mitzi. And he is your son Randolph – or Randy as you call him."

"I'm not calling him anything. You kids are phonies. You look nothing like the real Randy and Mitzi. What are you doing here?"

Just then my wife stepped into the kitchen. She was wearing a sky-blue Anrabess summer casual swing dress. She looked as fresh as a Forget Me Not. "They are waiting for you to take them to school," she said. "It's your day. I have my Breakfast Club."

"You don't fool me," I replied. "I ought to know my own children."

"Apparently you don't, dear. You seem awfully confused lately. The doctors are concerned. And so am I."

"You're concerned? How do you think I feel? Are our children dead?"

"Don't be silly. They are sitting right there across the table from you."

"Father, are you all right?" asked the wannabe Mitzi. Her face was a perfect mask of compassion.

"Of course, I'm not all right," I snapped. "Who are you?"

"That's enough," said my wife, gathering the children like a mother hen. "I will take them to school. Marilyn can chair today's Happy Housewives Breakfast Club. Today's speaker is Police Chief Bill Dozier, talking on the subject of 'Stranger Danger.' I was so looking forward to it."

"Are you taking these two little imposters to Morningside Elementary – or are you dropping them off at their acting class. They're not as adept in their roles as the first pair."

"Come, children," my wife ushered them out the door. "We don't want to be late for homeroom. Do you have your schoolbooks? Good. Come along quickly."

~ ~ ~

That night my wife didn't come home. Mrs. Mueller made me some soup, not a fancy meal. Her expression was stony cold. "What's the matter?" I probed.

"Well, sir, I hate to bring it up, but I haven't been paid in two months."

"Sorry, I thought my wife was taking care of the bills. I'll write you a check right now. I'm so embarrassed."

"Your wife –?"

"She's almost as forgetful as me. But I've got a good excuse." I tapped the side of my head. "Humpty Dumpty head, my wife calls it."

I scribbled my name on a check and handed it over. "Sir, I hate to do this, but I have to tender my resignation. I can't work here no more."

"What? You're the best housekeeper we've ever had."

"I'm the cook."

"I thought so, but my wife said –"

"I have to go," Mrs. Mueller said, gathering up her coat.

~ ~ ~

My wife was home when I got up the next morning. She was fussing over pancakes on an electric griddle. They smelled great.

"Where were you last night?" I asked, sliding into a chair at the table.

"With my cousins. I told you I was sleeping over."

No, she hadn't, but I didn't dispute her. I glanced at the empty seats around the table. "Where are the children?"

"What children?"

"Randy and Mitzi."

"Dear, we have no children. Randy and Mitzi are my cousins."

"Okay, okay, I don't want to argue. But what about those kids pretending to be our children?"

"Whatever are you talking about?"

"Those two kids you took to school yesterday morning."

"I didn't take any children to school. Your mind is playing tricks on you again. We need to get you another check-up with your doctor."

"But those kids –?"

"Dear, you're scaring me."

~ ~ ~

I never saw those two kids again. Or the first two. Or the real Randy and Mitzi. It was like none of them ever existed.

CHAPTER 10

Something had to be done. My wife had to go. This morning I slipped quietly out of bed and padded down to the garage and retrieved an ax. I'd bought it a couple of years ago to chop down a dead willow tree in the backyard. It still looked pretty sharp.

Stepping into the bedroom, I could see the shape of my wife under the covers. She had the sheets pulled over her head. Raising the ax, I brought it down swiftly on her head. But rather than the satisfying crack of metal striking bone, the blade sank deeply into a pillow, sending chunks of polyurethane foam swirling into the air.

"What are you doing?" came my wife's stern voice. "You just ruined a $59 MyPillow."

"Oops, sorry," I looked down at my handiwork. The pillow was ruined.

"And you've cut yourself. Your leg is bleeding."

I looked down at the blood dribbling down my calf. The ax had glanced off the coiled innards of the Posturepedic mattress and hit my leg. Damn, it was starting to hurt.

"What are you doing with that ax?" She looked anxious, her brow knitted, her green eyes squinted.

"Uh, trying to kill a mouse."

"There can't be a mouse in this house. Orkin services it quarterly."

"I swear I saw one," I lied.

"You probably saw Squishy."

"Squishy?"

"Our hamster. He got out of his cage last night. He's a clever little escape artist. I hope you haven't chopped him in half."

"We have a hamster?"

"Of course, we do. It belongs to the children."

~ ~ ~

The cut on my leg took eight stitches. Fortunately, it wasn't very deep. But I hurt like a sonuvagun.

The doctor at Midtown Walk-in Clinic asked me how I did it. I gave him some rambling story about cutting down a cherry tree. It made me sound like a latter-day George Washington. Ol' George who couldn't tell a lie. I hoped the doc would believe me too.

Limping to my car, I drove back to Morning Glory Drive. When I got there, I found that my wife had disappeared. I wasn't sure whether she had taken the kids to school, or gone to her Breakfast Club meeting. But how had she done that without the car?

Maybe it was time to buy a second car I told myself. Our old Taurus was on its last legs. It hadn't even got us to Deadman's Bend.

That reference to legs reminded me that my left leg hurt. Walking into the kitchen, I filled a glass with water and downed a handful of the pain pills the doctor had given me.

I slept the rest of the day.

Voice mail showed that Frederick Woolworth called three times, asking if I would be coming to work. He had papers for me to sign.

~ ~ ~

That night I fixed my own dinner. It was hard without Mrs. Mueller. I should try to hire her back, I told myself.

My wife got home later. There were no children in tow. "Where have you been?" I asked, trying to sound casual.

"Playing bridge. It's Thursday night."

"I thought you played bridge on Tuesday nights."

"No, it's always been Thursday."

"Oh, I lost track."

"You have a doctor's appointment tomorrow," she reminded me.

"I saw a doctor today," I said, pointing to the stitches on my calf.

"I'm talking about your neuropsychologist. He's part of the follow-up care from your coma."

"I don't like him. He confuses me. Tells me that I'm having delusions."

"You should listen to him, dear. A concussion is very serious. But, thank goodness, the MRI scans show no permanent brain damage."

"They said it's only a Grade 2 concussion. That's classified as moderate."

"While most people with a moderate TBI or concussion feel better within a couple of weeks, some will have symptoms for months or longer. You just have to give it time. You will get well."

"Do you really think so?"

"Absolutely." She gave me a reassuring kiss on the cheek.

"I hope so."

"Don't worry, dear. I will be here with you."

CHAPTER 11

That weekend my wife and I watched an old black-and-white movie on TCM called *Gaslight*. It starred Ingrid Bergman, one of my wife's all-time favorites. The movie told the story of a husband trying to drive his wife mad. But flickering gaslights and strange sounds in the attic were nothing compared to what I'm going through.

The more I thought about it, the more the movie's plot sounded familiar. Was my wife gaslighting me? Was all this business about my spells and confusion just a ruse to convince me that I'd lost my marbles?

Had she hired child actors to pretend they were Randy and Mitzi? That was possible, even if Silver Screen denied being behind it. And so had the Little Theater.

I was pretty sure we had two children – Little Ronnie and Mitzi. Why would she substitute doppelgängers for them, if not to make me think I'm crazy?

I would have to ask Mrs. Mueller about the children. She would know. I planned to hire her back, double her salary if I had to. The house was going to seed since she had left.

Mrs. Mueller was steady as a rock. She had been with us for years. I could trust her account of what was going on. She would know what happened to Ronnie and Mitzi, wouldn't she?

~ ~ ~

I told myself it was time to put a new plan into action. *Tempus fugit*, as the poet Virgil said. My wife had to die.

I remembered that book I'd seen in Klett's Reference Room, a thin volume titled *Fun With Electricity*. It said 411 people are accidentally electrocuted each year. Common place almost. There would be nothing suspicious about, say, my wife touching a stray wire on the fuse box or sticking a knife in the toaster to fish out a stuck slice of bread.

The question was, how to arrange it?

Right – I'm supposed to be the innovative genius. But I didn't have any practical ideas on how to pull this off. You can't just tie your wife up and stick her finger into a light socket.

Or can you?

No, I told myself, that wouldn't work. I'm not the physical type. Anything that involved subduing someone was way out of my league. No fisticuffs. No blunt objects. No Col. Mustard in the Library with a Lead Pipe.

I had to be more stealthy.

After all, the object was to kill my wife without getting caught. I had no suicidal impulses, no desire to spend the rest of my life in prison. I just wanted her to go away, to cease existing. To die.

I wished she would stop being so nice. That gets in the way of my working up the prerequisite anger and rage needed to complete this task. Everyone knows it's more difficult to kill a nice person. You can't empathize with your victim. Didn't all the books about serial killers say that? Or had I heard that on TV?

As I was shaving that morning, I glanced around at the bathtub. My wife loved to luxuriate in long hot baths. That reminded me of all those tales about people being electrocuted from dropping a hair dryer or a radio or some electrical implement into a tub of water. Stereotypical – but why wouldn't that work?

She usually reserved her tub time for Sunday nights. How difficult would it be to put a clock radio on an extension cord, tiptoe into the bathroom, and *ker-splash*! – the deed would be done!

However, this needed a little preparation.

We didn't have a clock radio. Should I go down to Walmart and buy one? No, that would look too suspicious, buying a radio on the same day it wound up in the bathtub. Maybe a hairdryer would be better. My wife already had several of those – a small one for travel, a standard issue hairdryer, and a large monstrosity that produced more air than a wind tunnel.

I settled on the middle one.

Next I found a tape measure in the kitchen junk drawer and trotted upstairs to measure the distance from the plug near the sink to the bathtub. Would the cord reach or did I need an extension? You have to be precise about these things.

Turned out, there was nothing to worry about. My measurements confirmed the dryer's cord was a six-footer, so that would work just fine.

Boy, was she going to be in for the shock of her life!

~ ~ ~

Around six, she announced, "I could use a good hot bath" as she disappeared up the steps. A few minutes later, I could hear the water running.

Approaching the bathroom door on tiptoes, I was stopped by my wife's whine: "Dear, the hot water ran out. Could you please check the water heater? Or maybe the fuse box?"

I scrambled back down the steps and called up, "Sure thing, hon." I hope my hard breathing wasn't obvious. My heart was doing rapid little pit-a-pats. I'd almost got caught sneaking up on her, hair dryer in hand.

Best to get the hot water going. Else she would never get into the tub. So I stepped into the adjoining garage where the fuse box was located and pulled open the metal door.

Zz-zkt!

I was knocked on my butt by an electoral shock.

When I woke up, a paramedical with sad brown eyes and a five-o'clock shadow was looking down at me. "Take it easy, pal," he said. "You're gonna be all right. But you've got your wife to thank for that. If she hadn't been here to give you CPR ...." He let the words trail off.

CHAPTER 12

"**H**ear you had a scare at home," said Frederick Woolworth that Monday morning. He looked at me with sad brown eyes – much like that paramedic's – and patted me consolingly on the arm. "Gotta watch out. For an inventor, you're not much of a handyman."

"Guess not," I allowed. No need to go into the subject further. I had been nearly killed, and my wife was surely behind it. How else could a live wire have gotten in that fuse box?

Did this mean mutual warfare, each trying to do in the other? Had she figured out my plot and decided to fight back? Was she now a threat?

Randy – the lab assistant, not my wife's cousin or our son – was busy at the workbench. He was messing around with one of our rejected ideas, a squirt gun for picnics that delivered mustard, ketchup, or mayonnaise with the turn of a dial. First time we tried it, I'm told, the barrel kept clogging up. This time around, Randy was trying a wider barrel and thinner condiments. I figured it wouldn't work because consumers wanted thick ketchup, not a watery red sauce.

Mitzi was doing whatever it was that Mitzi did. Reading a paperback, it looked like. The title was kind of lurid – *Seven Inches of Paradise*. She claimed it was the instruction manual for a new back massager she had purchased over the weekend.

That got me thinking. After discarding several tamer ideas, I settled on a massager designed to stimulate the g-spot.

Everybody liked that brainstorm, the first acceptable idea I had come up with since the bomb incident.

"I'd buy one," volunteered Mitzi.

"Too much information," I replied hastily.

"This will sell," my partner declared.

"I'll get started on a design right away," said Randy. "Maybe Mitzi can help me get the measurement right."

Without confirming her assistance, she held up her book, displaying the cover: *Seven Inches of Paradise*. A hint as to the desired length.

I rolled my eyes and went into my office and shut the door. Gay, my foot. Ride sharing, you bet. I still wasn't sure about those two. Something was going on between them.

Frederick Woolworth knocked quietly on my door, then let himself in. "Glad to see you're getting back to your old self," he told me. "We've been through a long dry spell. We were running out of old ideas to play with. Usually, there was a good reason we discarded them in the first place."

I had to admit, my success felt gratifying. Dopamine was raging through my brain. Oxytocin, serotonin, and endorphins joined them, completing the happy-making D.O.S.E. that scientists talk about.

"Feels good to be back," I replied in a meek voice. Trying to show my humble side.

Then he said, "But a word of advice, you've got to stop talking about your wife to Randy and Mitzi. It's downright creepy."

That stopped me. "How is talking about my wife creepy? You talk about your wife all the time."

"Yeah, but in your case it's different."

"Different, how?"

"You know," he said and left the room.

~ ~ ~

How had my partner heard about my mishap with the fuse box? Had my wife called him? I hadn't told anybody about it ... well, except Marty Kovaks at the newspaper kiosk down the street. This morning I'd stopped there for my monthly copy of *Inventers Omnibus*. Hard to find, he specially ordered the magazine for me. I may have mentioned my encounter with the fuse box to him. I couldn't remember for sure.

Perhaps Frederick had stopped there for his *Daily Telegraph*. Marty might have mentioned it. My partner always picked up his newspapers at the kiosk. Klett's Bookstore was too far out of the way. Me, I opted for home delivery. The service was much better here in town.

I liked that theory better than the thought that Frederick might be talking with my wife behind my back. But then, their collaboration would explain all this confusion over the multiple Randy's and Mitzi's.

~ ~ ~

That night I got a second chance. My wife stretched her arms and said, I think I'm going to take a long hot bath."

"Too bad we don't have a jacuzzi ... or better still, a hot tub," I commented, just making conversation.

She seized on the suggestion. "That's a great idea, John. Let's go shopping this coming Saturday. Peter Paul's Pool & Patio Pavilion carries hot tubs. I've seen then when driving past."

"Sure," I said. "Now go enjoy your bath. Maybe I'll come up and wash your back."

"Hmm, that would be nice."

I watched her go up the stairs, my mind racing. Was that hairdryer still plugged in? Or had she put it away? If so, where?

Listening to the water running in the bathroom, I searched our bedroom until I located the medium-sized hairdryer in a bureau drawer. My wife had an orderly streak. *A place for everything, and everything in its place*, she liked to say.

Standing outside the bathroom door, I could hear her humming and sloshing about. Better wait till she settled down and relaxed. If I timed it right, she might doze off in the tub. She often did that.

I used to think that a lot of rock stars died in airplane crashes – Buddy Holly, Patsy Cline, Jim Reeves, Otis Redding, Jim Croce, Lynyrd Skynyrd, Stevie Ray Vaughan, Rick Nelson, *et al*. But now I was starting to think bathtubs were equally dangerous, given the number of famous people who had met their demise in them – Whitney Houston, Bobbi Kristina

Brown, Jim Morrison, Sridevi, Orville Redenbacher, Claude Francois, Aaron Carter, *etc.*

After about fifteen minutes the humming stopped, making me think she had fallen asleep. I waited another ten minutes just to be sure, watching the minute hand on my Cartier Baignoire wristwatch. The watch seemed appropriate. The Cartier Baignoire was designed for Grand Duchess Vladimir of Russia in 1912. For this, Louis Cartier took a traditional round watch and stretched it out, forming the oval shape of a bathtub ("baignoire" in French) – hence its name.

Easing the door open, I stepped into the marble-tiled room with the hairdryer in hand. One glance told me my wife was asleep. It would be so easy to push her head under the water and hold it down till she drowned. But that was too physical for me. What if she struggled? Even if I succeeded, she might claw me, leaving marks that would be difficult to explain to police.

Better stick to the plan.

Plugging in the hairdryer, I switched it on to make sure it had an electrical current flowing through it. The handheld unit gave me a soft purr in return, air whistling out of its blunt spout.

Ready to go.

Quickly, I turned and tossed the electromechanical device into the foamy bath water. There was a popping sound – *spt!* *spt!* – and then all the lights in the house went out. The hairdryer had shorted out, flipping the main switch in the fuse box in the garage. Hopefully, enough electricity had hit the water to do the job.

I sniffed. I could smell lavender and soap and burnt flesh – at least, that's what I told myself. The smell was cloying. I stepped into the hallway to avoid gagging.

I had my iPhone with me. Dialing 9-1-1, I said, "I'd like to report an accident."

CHAPTER 13

Taking a deep breath, I walked down the stairs to wait for the police. The house was dark, so I was careful to place one foot in front of the other, keeping my hand tightly on the railing. My breath was slowly returning to normal. Everything was quiet – "not a creature was stirring, not even a mouse," as the old Clement Clarke Moore poem goes.

I bumped my way along the dark hallway, heading toward the kitchen. As I recalled, there were candles in a cabinet drawer. Turning the corner, I was taken up short. There was a glow emanating from the kitchen. What the –?

"Hi, dear," came a familiar voice. My wife stood there in a bathrobe, holding a flickering candle in each hand.

"But you –"

"My bath was too hot. While I was waiting for it to cool, the lights went out. So I came down here to get some candles."

"Yeah, I came down here to get a candle myself."

A siren sounded in the distance.

"The police," I said. "I called them."

"Why?"

"Uh, I thought we might have a burglar. That someone had cut the power line."

"Don't be silly. We've been having a problem with our fuse box."

"I know, I know. Last time, I almost got electrocuted."

The siren was closer.

"Oh my, I don't want the police to see me like this – in a bathrobe, no makeup. I'm going next door to my friend Marilyn's house. You handle this."

"Uh, sure."

I heard the backdoor slam just as a police cruiser pulled into the driveway, its light bar flashing *red, blue, red, blue*. Thirty seconds later, there was a loud banging on the front door and a voice shouting, "Police!"

Officer Ed Johnson – as his shiny gold nametag identified him – was the same cop who had shown up when I'd "accidentally" poisoned myself. He gave me that "What now?" look.

"My lights went out. I heard someone upstairs. Thought it might be an intruder."

The policeman sighed. "Okay, let's take a look." He was carrying a powerful TK-30 flashlight that cast a wide beam. He didn't bother taking out his revolver, a sign that he didn't put much stock in the burglar story.

"This way," I led him up the carpeted steps. "I think someone might be in the bathroom. That's the first door at the top."

Th cop opened the bathdoor carefully, sticking his head inside, sweeping the flash around the room – blue marble tile, gleaming white porcelain, silvery fixtures. "Uh-oh," he said. "You don't want to come in here."

"Why not?"

"Your dog's dead. Looks like he knocked over a hairdryer, slipped and fell into the tub, got himself barbecued. Sorry about that."

"I had filled the tub to take a bath, but got distracted. Rex was roaming around up here."

"Rex?"

"The dog. He belonged to my children."

"Didn't know you had children."

"They are off visiting my wife's cousins."

"Oh, right. Your wife –" He turned toward the stairs. "Guess I better get going. No burglar here. I'm not even gonna write up a report on this. Sorry again about your dog."

CHAPTER 14

If I had children, it occurred to me, they would have bedrooms in the house. But a casual walkaround confirmed there were no children's rooms in the two-story Georgian. No wonder I couldn't remember any rooms with rainbows or planets and stars. The answer was obvious: My wife and I had no children.

But then, who were Randy and Mitzi? Maybe the names *did* belong to my wife's cousins. No, wait – Randy and Mitzi worked at Wonder Works. How had I become so confused?

Then I had another thought. What if I was right about the bomb killing my kids. Maybe when my wife had the living room repaired, she'd at the same time converted the children's bedrooms to a study and a sewing room. Getting rid of the sad memories of her dead son and daughter. That could explain the lack of children's bedrooms.

But I didn't want to think like that.

I shook my head to clear it. Like a dog shaking off water.

Poor Rex.

My wife had gone to stay with her cousins, whatever their names were. I'd hired a cleaning crew to haul away the remains of the dog and sanitize the bathroom. The fuse box was easy; the lights had been restored within minutes. Everything was back to "normal."

Or so I hoped.

At work, I didn't mention the incident. I didn't need more of those sympathetic looks from my partner. I needed to focus on coming up with more projects. Sales were falling off, affected by our failure to introduce any new products.

There wasn't anything I could do about killing my wife as long as she was visiting her cousins. I didn't even know where they lived. Whenever I asked, she had vaguely said, "Across town," with an amorphous wave of the hand.

It was kind of lonely at home without Rex. I was surprised how much I missed his presence, a shaggy yellow companion with wagging tail. Dogs are good company. It wasn't clear how Rex wound up in that bathtub; my wife claimed she'd been giving him a bath. But I could swear I'd seen her in the tub just seconds before I tossed that hairdryer. How could she have gotten out so fast?

So far, my attempts to rid myself of my wife hadn't gone well. Maybe I was being "too clever" – a curse for inventors. It was time to take on the task in a more direct way. I went shopping for a gun.

~ ~ ~

Bob's Pawn Shop & Gun Depot had more bars on its windows than a jail. The front door was made of thick metal and you had to be buzzed in. Bob was an ex-Desert Storm vet who believed in every man's right to own an AR-15 ... or even a Sherman tank. His buzz cut made his head look like a skull. His once-muscled body had gone to fat. He wore baggy trousers and a brownish wife-beater undershirt like you'd see in the military. A tattoo on his shoulder proclaimed *SEMPER FI*. He greeted me with a toothy smile that reminded me of a wolf.

"What can I do for you today? Pawn a ring? Sell you some ammo? Sign you up for the NRA?"

"Uh, I need a gun."

"You came to the right place," he waved his meaty arm at a wall displaying military-style semi-automatic rifles. "We have a fine selection of sporting rifles."

"I'm looking a pistol."

"Revolver or semi-auto?"

"The difference?"

"A semi holds more bullets." A practical view.

"One or two shots should do the trick."

"A revolver then." He pointed to a glass case. "These are on sale – today only. Colts, Smith & Wesson, Charter Arms."

Pursing my lips, I pretended to study the weapons like I knew what I was looking at. "Which do you recommend?"

"How about a medium caliber, a .32? Here's a Ruger H&R Magnum, a six-shooter."

"Hmm, the barrel's too long. Something smaller?" I wanted to be able to conceal it, if need be.

"Then this Charter Arms snub-nose is the one for you. A two-inch barrel, stainless steel frame, holds six rounds. Today, only $400 cash."

"Cash?"

"You don't have it on you, I've got an ATM over there in the corner."

"Okay, I'll take it and a box of bullets."

"Coming right up. Here's some paperwork you have to fill out." He shoved a clipboard holding a sheaf of official forms across the glass counter.

"Wrap it up," I nodded.

"Oh, you can't take it with you. There's a waiting period, you know."

"I can't take it with me?" My wife was due home this afternoon.

"Sorry, that's the law."

"Oh."

Bob leaned forward and lowered his voice. "We do have workarounds for an extra hundred."

"That sounds fair."

"We'll backdate your application. And I got a way around the background check. Don't worry about it."

"Thanks. By the way, how does this pistol work?"

"Simple. I'll load it for you. Remington hollow points, that will stop most anything. Then, when you want to use the pistol, just point and pull the trigger. That's all there is to it."

"What if I miss?"

"Pull the trigger again. You got six tries before you have to reload it. But up close, it's hard to miss."

CHAPTER 15

No need to wait. My wife should be home by now. Pulling my new Charter Arms Undercoverette Model 73220 from under my coat, I rushed into the house, charged up the stairs, and burst into the bedroom where my wife was brushing her hair.

Ka-bam! *Ka-bam*!

At close range, I fired two rounds into her head. Her cranium splattered like a watermelon, all red and squishy. No way she wiggled out of this one.

Turning, I retraced my steps out the front door and jumped into my Ford Taurus. Pausing a minute to catch my breath, I started up the car (I had replaced the battery last week) and raced away. I planned to leave an anonymous 9-1-1 call to the police, reporting gunfire on my block. Let them find my wife's body.

But first, I needed to get rid of the gun. Once ditched, no one could trace the .32 to me. For an extra $500, Bob of Bob's Pawn Shop & Gun Depot had kept the transaction off the books. The gun would be reported as stolen.

A half mile from my house, I pulled over at a construction site on Hollyhock Terrace. Beater cars and a Ford F-150 pickup that said SWANSON CONSTRUCTION INC. on the door panel were parked around the site like a low-rent used car lot. The yard was all sand and dirt covered by tire tracks, grass to be planted later.

"Hi, Jim," I called out to a man in dusty coveralls. "How's the job going?"

"On schedule," answered Jim Swanson, owner of Swanson Construction. He was my best friend and I often stopped by to check the progress on his new houses. Somehow, I remember that.

"We're doing the foundation today," he continued, waving toward a big truck with a rotating drum on the back. Workmen surrounded the mixer, guiding the pasty gray cement down a chute that emptied into a neatly dug trench.

"Mind if I have a look?"

"Nothing to see, but help yourself," Jim Swanson shrugged.

Stepping forward, I bent over the trench to look. The cement was pouring into it like a pastry chef icing a cake. Turning, I pointed toward the street and shouted, "Look, a naked lady!"

All the workers swiveled their heads to look.

"Where?"

"A naked lady?"

"I don't see her."

"Where is she?"

Amid the confusion, I dropped the Charter Arms revolver into the muck in the trench. The gun disappeared into the depths of the cement. No one would ever find that.

"Just kidding," I said. "Gotta go. Thanks for the progress report."

There were shouts of disappointment as I crawled into my Taurus and turned the ignition. Some of the names they called me were rude. My friend Jim was chuckling, as if I'd pulled a great joke on his crew. Construction men have a strange sense of humor.

~ ~ ~

When I got to Wonder Works, I made a point of looking over Randy's progress with the reengineering of the g-spot massager. Mitzi had complained that the motor got too heated for such a delicate operation. "Smaller motor, heat shield, that should do the trick," explained Randy, proud of his work.

I nodded my approval.

Randy was good. If I ever needed to reverse engineer a flying saucer's alien technology, he would be my first choice to assist. I would even put up with Mitzi if that's what it took.

Frederick Woolworth stepped out of his office. "Where have you been all day? You need to sign some papers. That condiment gun for picnics, we've got a buyer. An outright sale to Monument Toys."

"Had some errands to run."

"Well, come along. Get out your pen."

~ ~ ~

It took a while before I could make that 9-1-1 call. I couldn't do it from the office, where my phone number would show up on the police dispatcher's screen. Making an excuse about "picking up a prescription," I drove across town to Harlow's Hardware and Lumber. As I expected, no one was at the customer service desk, so I reached across the counter, picked up the phone, dialed the three digits, and reported a "shots fired," as they say on TV cop shows.

Then I hurried back to work and occupied myself for the rest of the afternoon with Randy and the prototype massager. I got no calls.

But when I got home, a police cruiser with flashing lights was parked on the street cattycornered to my house. It was hard to tell which house interested him, all the residences looking alike, Georgian designs lined up like peas in a pod. Only subtle shades of pastel distinguished one from the other. Morning Glory Drive was part of a high-end development project, the cookie-cutter houses going for half-a-mil each.

As I pulled into the driveway, the policeman sauntered over. I recognized him as Officer Ed Johnson. I wondered if he was assigned to this neighborhood ... or to me? Rolling down the window, I called out, "What's going on?"

"Your neighbor has been killed."

"My neighbor –?"

"Marilyn Zephyr. The house on the left." He indicated a Georgian that was the mirror image of mine, same pukey green, same yellow curtains in the window. I remembered that

Marilyn and my wife had gone shopping together, buying the same lemony voile curtains. They had been good friends.

This news that Marilyn Zephyr had been murdered was staggering. What kind of coincidence was it that my wife and my next-door neighbor would both get knocked off on the same day?

The fact that Officer Johnson was only talking about Marilyn's death made me think he hadn't discovered my wife's body yet. What should I do – go in the house and then shout out that I'd discovered my wife dead too? That might, in fact, be a good strategy, let them think a serial killer had struck the neighborhood. That ought to take some of the heat off me as a suspect. I had no reason to kill Marilyn Zephyr.

"Well, I'd better go inside and let you get back to solving this horrendous crime," I said, climbing out of the Taurus.

As I started up the brick walkway, Officer Johnson called out, "Hold on, sir. I can't let you do that."

"Uh, why not?"

"Because we have a witness who claims she saw you go into the Zephyr house earlier today carrying a pistol. I'm afraid I'm going to have to place you under arrest."

"Me? That's crazy. Maybe she saw me going into my house earlier. All the houses on the street look alike. And I was carrying a new product we're testing, a gun-looking device that squirts mustard onto your hot dog at a picnic. I'm an inventor, you know."

"Yes, I'm familiar with your work. You're the guy who came up with the robot dog-walker. I really liked that one.

Wish I could afford one for my mutt."

"Clear up this misunderstanding and I will send you a dozen."

Officer Johnson shook his head with a tight smile. "Sorry, sir, but I can't take a bribe."

"Not a bribe. A gift."

"Perhaps you'd better come downtown with me. We'll book you – photo, fingerprints, a phone call to your lawyer – and you'll get to spend the night in a holding cell. They will probably bring you before a magistrate in the morning to hear your side of the story."

"Uh, could I go inside and get a change of underwear and a toothbrush?"

"Not supposed to do that, but since it's you –"

"Thanks," I said and led him into the house. "Stuff's in my bedroom at the top of the stairs."

"I remember the way from when your dog got himself zapped in the bathtub."

"Yeah, poor Rex," I said, climbing the stairs wearily.

At the landing, I faced the door to the bedroom. Inside awaited my wife's bloody corpse. Maybe that would throw some confusion into this crazy accusation that I'd killed my neighbor. "Here we are," I announced, pushing open the door as if a surprise birthday party waited inside. The heavy oak door swung inward to reveal ...

... nothing.

The bed was perfectly made (thanks to Mrs. Mueller, I assume). The carpet looked freshly vacuumed. There were fresh flowers on the nightstand. But no blood-splattered dead body.

Even Mrs. Mueller could not have so sparklingly cleaned up all that gore. My wife's head had exploded, blood flying everywhere. I stared google-eyed at the pristine scene. Where was my wife's corpse?

Then it hit me: Maybe my wife was the dead body next door, not Marilyn Zephyr. With her head blown off, she would be difficult to identify. No face, no dental records. But what had she been doing next door? I was sure I shot her in *our* bedroom.

"What's the matter?" asked Officer Johnson. "You look like you've seen a ghost."

"No," I said. "That's the problem, I didn't see a ghost."

CHAPTER 16

No way was I going downtown with Officer Ed Johnson. Witness or no witness, I hadn't shot Marilyn Zephyr. They weren't going to pin that on me.

As for my wife, guilty as charged. But she had deserved it, so I wasn't going to take the heat for that one either. Maybe I wouldn't have to, I told myself. There was no body (explain that). No gun to be found (thanks to Swanson Construction). No evidence at all.

After the police fully investigated, I would be cleared. But I needed time to let that to happen. I needed to ditch Officer Johnson, and lay low for a few days. Let it sort itself out.

But how?

Fortunately, the cop hadn't cuffed me. And I was here in my own bedroom. So I had a few tricks up my sleeve. Don't forget, I *am* an inventor.

Like many homes in this area, we had a panic room, a safe harbor from home invasions and such. Our panic room was located in the basement, a concrete bunker that was all but impenetrable. All I had to do was get from here to there.

No problem.

"Let me grab that change of underwear," I said, walking to a closet door. Opening it nonchalantly, I stepped inside ... and vanished.

"What just happen?" exclaimed Officer Johnson, as bewildered as if he'd just watched David Copperfield make an elephant disappear.

~ ~ ~

For the panic room in the basement, I had installed one of those tubular slides like you see at school playgrounds. It curved through the innards of the house, depositing its load onto a mattress. Down I slid like Alice going down the rabbit hole, looping around like a corkscrew. It made me dizzy.

Whomp!

When I landed, the impact knocked the breath out of me. I lay there a few seconds, getting oriented. I hadn't been down here in the panic room since before my concussion.

The room was pitch black except for a couple of night lights. I could make out the couch and a table and a pantry cabinet. Like a living room with no windows. I knew the couch could be folded out to make a bed. And that the pantry was stocked with Mountain Home survival food, enough for two weeks. If you had to hide out in here for more than two weeks, you were already screwed. Also, there was a wall phone, pre-programmed to 9-1-1.

One other thing: I had stashed ten grand in a go-bag. Just in case I needed to flee ... like now. Retrieving the wad of money, I counted it to make sure it was all there. Yep, right down to the last $100 bill.

Now you may think of my being in this panic room was like a rat in a trap. That I would be holed up here until the cops busted in. But not so. Any hidey-hole needs a backdoor.

And I had one.

Opening the pantry, I unloaded the cannisters of survival food to lighten the load, then I slid the bulky cabinet away from the wall. Behind it was a hole big enough to crawl through. A corrugated metal pipe led into the darkness. The exit was a hidden manhole in the middle of Marilyn Zephyr's rose garden. I wiggled out, clutching my go-bag.

~ ~ ~

By sunset I had made it to the foot of 102's climb up to Deadman's Bend. I'd kept to the sidewalks, strolling along like a man out for an evening sojourn. I wished I'd still had Rex, for a man walking a dog would be even less suspicious.

My ears were attuned for any sirens, but no police cars passed me during the entire distance I'd covered. Guess the search was confined to my neighborhood. First, they would have to locate the panic room and break in. Then find the escape hatch (I'd pulled the pantry back into place). And then make sure I wasn't hiding in the backyards of nearby homes.

You'd think they would have put up roadblocks on the two roads leading out of the valley, but 102 was as open as a raceway.

I didn't want to get caught going up the steep hill. There was little foliage lining the road, no place to hide from passing cars. Instead, I veered along the base of the plateau until I found the crevice that led to the gorge below Deadman's Bend. It was a popular hiking path, but not during hot days in the summer. I didn't encounter a single person.

When I came to the rocky field, going got a lot harder, having to circle around boulders and climb over granite outcroppings. Wish I'd had the shoes for it. What I would have given for a good pair of Nike Pegasus walking shoes or L.L. Bean hiking boots!

My calf was throbbing, the stitches strained from all the walking. But they held.

Looking around the gorge, the only remnants I saw of Marlon Klett's school bus was a headlamp laying there like a glass eyeball and that fold-out metal sign that says STOP. Jim Swanson had done a good job with his big XCMG XGC88000 heavy lift crawler crane. For lifting the bus out of the gorge, he'd charged me more than I'd paid as restitution to Marlon Klett. But town ordinances said the wreckage had to be removed. In effect, bad drivers were required to clean up after themselves.

At the far end of the gorge was a narrow crevice with a trail leading up to the pasture behind Klett's Bookstore. The back door to this rat trap, so to speak. But I couldn't find it. Finally, I figured out that it had been covered up by a rock slide.

No way out.

That meant I'd have to backtrack, make my way across the jagged boulder field the way I had come. The only way up to

Klett's would be Highway 102, but by now it was likely crawling with cops. This was a bummer.

So I sat down on a rock to think. And to rest. I was exhausted from all my hiking. I wasn't used to strenuous activity. Since that concussion I'd barely been outdoors. And I'm certainly not a gym rat.

My stomach was rumbling like locomotive. I wished I'd been smart enough to bring some water and food.

"Like a locomotive" … that thought reminded me of the abandoned train track that ran along the plateau opposite Deadman's Bend. A railway bridge had spanned a short gap in the rim. Hadn't I heard someone say that it had collapsed from age and neglect?

By now it was too dark to see much. I didn't fancy stumbling along in this boulder field without a flashlight. I thought I had included one in the go-bag, but I couldn't find it.

I ate the two energy bars from the go-bag. Some of the other items seemed useless – fish hooks, a plastic pee jar, an N95 face mask with extra filters, safety pins, a pack of playing cards, a hairbrush – so I dumped them to lighten the load. Useful items in the bag included a Ka-Bar knife, compass, first aid kit, a tactical folding shovel, nylon cord, a heavy duty space blanket, insect spray, a hand-crank digital radio, extra underwear, and a roll of toilet paper.

I wondered if there were snakes out here. Wouldn't rocks offer a rattlesnake a good place to hide from the overhead sun? Did they come out at night? The thought made me shiver. I gripped the Ka-Bar knife like a warrior ready to do battle. But nothing was moving among the rocks.

Spraying myself with insect repellent, I tried the radio but couldn't pick up a signal. Tossing it aside, I searched for any other useful items. One of these was a solar charger for my iPhone, so I tossed it back in the go-bag. Another was a stainless steel water bottle, but it was empty. Also, I found a glow stick but I was afraid to use it for the light might be visible from Deadman's Bend.

Rolling up my coat to make a pillow, I stretched out on a flat slab of rock, wrapped myself in the silvery space blanket, and tried to sleep. The night was warm, the temperature about 70°. Eventually I abandoned the space blanket. It was hard to get comfortable. The rigid surface of the rock hurt my back. This was a long way from the Posturepedic on my king-size bed back home. I could tell it was going to be a long night.

~ ~ ~

The sun woke me up. My throat felt parched. My back ached like a whiplash victim. Staring upward I could see a cloudless blue sky and the lip of the cliff at Deadman's Bend. The guardrail had been replaced, the metal gleaming like silver in the morning sunlight. I could hear cars up there on 102, commuters on their way to work down in the valley. That left me feeling vulnerable. Might someone spot me down here, stretched out on a rock at the bottom of the gorge?

Scrambling off the slab, I made my way over to the shadow of the cliff where I would be hidden from above. How to get out of this fishbowl, I asked myself? Then I remembered the collapsed railway bridge.

Across the gorge I could see what looked like the remnants of a giant Erector set. The crisscross of the tracks climbed up the face of the opposite cliff like the rungs of a ladder My way out, I said to myself. Grabbing my go-bag, I started making my way across the rocks toward the ruined railings. For some reason, I began humming "Stairway to Heaven."

Climbing up the tracks was dangerous. Many of the sleepers – those crossbeam supports for the rails – were loose, coming off under my weight. I should have stuck to that diet. I'd tried the Keto for a while, but dropped off it because I missed McDonald's French fries.

As I neared the top, a weak sleeper board cracked, leaving my feet dangling in midair. My grip wasn't very secure, splinters biting into the palms of my hands. My feet peddled, seeking purchase, like I was riding an invisible bicycle. Making the mistake of looking down, I could see the sharp rocks in the gorge below. Not having eaten, my stomach was gurgling and turning – maybe out of hunger, maybe out of fear.

One hand slipped off the thick sleeper; the other holding on by the tips of my fingers. I was surely going to die, I told myself in a panic. Swinging my free hand around, it slapped against the iron rail. I grabbed it and with a sudden shift wrapped myself around the rail as if climbing a tree. I hugged it for all I was worth.

Now what? I asked myself.

Keep going up because I can't go down. Reaching out, I got a better grip on the sleeper above my head and with a Herculean effort chinned myself up. Swinging my leg over the crossbeam, I leveraged myself up until I was straddling it like sitting on a saddle horse.

Resting there for a while, I let my pulse return to normal. My muscles ached. In college, I liberally used Absorbine Jr. after every gym class. I would have given a year's salary for a bottle of that topical pain reliever right now.

Once I had rested, I set off again, climbing up the rails like a ladder, from sleeper to sleeper, eyes focused on the approaching rim of the cliff.

Probably I got overconfident, for when I tried to step off the railroad tracks onto the rocky edge of the cliff, my foot slipped and I tumbled backward, careening toward the abyss. Down, down, down. Believe it or not, I suddenly jerked to a stop, my coat having snagged on an iron spike. I swung there in the air, like a ham hanging in a smoke house, the coat bunched against my armpits. Thank God, I told myself. Then I heard the coat begin to rip.

R-p-p-p-p-p!

Grabbing a sleeper, I once again shifted onto body of the railway track. Just in time. I shucked my ruined coat and resumed my climb. This time, I was more careful stepping over onto the rim of the cliff.

CHAPTER 17

In the distance I could see an unpainted three-story building – Klett's Bookstore. I was amazed he could make a living selling mostly used books in a location this far out of town. There were no sidewalks along 102, a dangerous highway to traverse. His business had no walk-in traffic. The bookstore's customers were destination-oriented drivers. He sold a lot of morning papers and lurid paperbacks.

Remembering that Marlon Klett had banned me for life, I wasn't sure what kind of greeting I could expect. Estelle Bennington was a kind-hearted soul, always nurturing fallen birds and stray kittens, but she still had her partner to answer to. Marlon just might call the cops, so I had to approach this very carefully.

I knew that the bookstore – a former boarding house – had lots of spare rooms, a perfect place for me to hide out. Practically in plain sight, but the police would never think of looking here. What's more, Marlon's temper was legendary. Local cops didn't want to deal with that.

How to convince Marlon Klett to take me in? Money was my best bet. Maybe I should offer to buy him and Estelle roundtrip tickets to the Grand Canyon. I had about $300,000 in my bank account. Apparently, some of my previous inventions had done very well. That gave me a bankroll to play with – if I could get at it.

Being a fugitive on the run, I couldn't just walk into Sunrise Savings & Loan and make a withdrawal. And it would take over a year and a half to withdraw it from an ATM, $500 at a time. And I doubted Marlon Klett would take a check.

I sat there in the tall grass, waiting for the right moment to approach the bookstore building. Best to keep low till there were no customers there. I counted three cars in the lot.

My stomach was growling again. I could have eaten a handful of dirt. I hoped Klett's Bookstore had some donuts left to go with that Maxwell House coffee. I could barely think of anything other than those sticky sweet glazed wheels of leavened fried dough.

Next to me I spotted a mushroom. The large fungus displayed a domed white cap on an off-white stem. I wondered if it might be edible. But when I looked more closely I realized it was an *Amanita phalloides*, commonly known as the Death Cap mushroom. I recognized it from that book I'd seen at Klett's Bookshop, the one titled *Poisonous Mushrooms to Avoid*. Considered the world's most poisonous mushroom, the *A. phalloides* is responsible for 90% of all mushroom-related fatalities.

No meal here, but maybe it would come in handy. I might try treating my wife to a very special dinner, steak smothered in mushrooms. Yummy for her. Wrapping some of my toilet paper around the fat cap, I carefully plucked it and dropped the fungus into my go-bag.

But I was still hungry.

Trying to focus on something else, I wondered whether my wife was dead or alive. I was sure I had blasted her head off. But there was no sign of any such carnage in our bedroom. Was it possible I'd shot Marilyn Zephyr by mistake?

That seemed possible, the more I considered it. In my haste, had I run into the wrong house – they all looked alike – and shot the wrong woman in the wrong bedroom?

If so, that meant my wife was still alive. I would need to circle back to the house and kill her. Maybe this time, I would bludgeon her. Up close and personal, as they say. That way there would be no question that she was dead. I had a baseball bat that I kept in the hall closet for protection – in case an unwanted invader showed up at my front door. That would do the job.

But that would have to wait. I was too hot right now to show my face down in the valley. I needed to lay low for a while, see how Marilyn Zephyr's murder investigation played out. Maybe they would catch the real killer –assuming I didn't do it. Find some fingerprints or DNA or a security video. I'd have to be patient.

~ ~ ~

Around 10 o'clock, according to my Cartier wristwatch, there was a lull at the bookstore up the hill. The last car pulled away, climbing the steep driveway onto Highway 102. I'd better get moving before another customer showed up.

Trying to keep low, I ran bent-over through the tall grass toward the gabled building. If Marlon spotted me, he might call the police before I even got to the front porch. Rounding the corner of the house, I leaped onto the porch and pushed my way through the front door. Marlon and Estelle were behind the counter, looking over a travel brochure. Their heads snapped up, mouths gaping open in surprise.

"Don't panic," I shouted. "I come here in peace." That sounded a little dorky, like an alien stepping out of a spaceship on the White House lawn, but that was the best I could do on short notice.

"John, what are you doing here?" said Estelle, regaining her composure. She was always more calm than Marlon.

"I need a place to hide out for a few days – till the police clear up Marilyn Zephyr's murder."

"Are you crazy?" said Marlon. "You're a wanted criminal. I'm not going to be an accessory to murder. Besides, I liked Mrs. Zephyr."

"Now, now, calm down," shushed Estelle, patting his arm as if trying to soothe a wild stallion.

"Look, I'm innocent," I pleaded. "You know me, know my wife. Do I look like some mad-dog killer?"

"Yes," declared Marlon. "Your hair is sticking up like a porcupine. Your shirt is ripped. Your pants are covered in dirt. You look like you slept in the bushes last night."

"That's practically true," I admitted. "I spent the night down in the gorge. Are there snakes down there?"

"Lots of 'em," grunted the bookstore owner. "Poisonous too."

That gave me another idea about how to kill my wife, but I didn't have time to think about it now. "Will you let me hide out in one of your upstairs rooms for a couple of days? If the police haven't solved the murder by then, I swear I'll turn myself in."

"Well –" began Estelle.

"No way," Marlon cut her off.

"Please. I will pay you. A hundred thousand dollars."

"John, we couldn't take your money," said Estelle.

"Yes, we could," interjected her common law husband. "A hundred grand, you say?"

"Right. Just as soon as I can get to the bank."

"Ha! I knew there was a catch. Estelle, call the police. Tell 'em to come pick up their fugitive."

"Two hundred," I said.

Marlon's eyes seemed to bulge. "Two hundred grand?"

"Cash. Unreported. Our secret."

"Do we still have to wait till you can get to the bank without getting arrested?"

"I'm afraid so."

"Hmm, I might be willing to consider that. I can be patient, particularly if you sign an IOU."

"You got it," I nodded. "Hand me a pen."

~ ~ ~

I ate all the glazed donuts, four in all. And drank three cups of coffee. That left me pretty wired, but when Estelle

Bennington led me to a room on the far corner of the second floor I plopped onto the feather bed and instantly fell asleep.

When I woke up, my Cartier wristwatch told me it was 4 in the afternoon. There was a tray of baloney sandwiches, ice tea, and coconut cake waiting on a side table. I ate every scrap in one setting. My tummy had quit growling.

Tiptoeing down the bare wooden stairs, careful just in case there were customers in the store, I came upon Marlon and Estelle having an argument.

"Call the police," Marlon was saying.

"You agreed to take his two hundred thousand dollars. And he signed an IOU. That's a contract, Marlon."

"I was just stalling for time. He's a dangerous criminal. Our lives might be in danger."

"Posh," she dismissed his words. "John needs our help. And we promised to give him shelter for two or three days."

"For money."

"Then why are you going back on your word?"

"I don't trust him. He wrecked my bus."

"And he paid you for it. Probably more than that old rust bucket was worth."

"He agreed to the price."

"And *you* agreed to the price he offered us to stay here."

"That is a lot of money. If I thought we'd ever see it, I'd let him stay."

About then I stepped forward. "You will see it," I promised. "I'm a man of my word."

"Marlon is too," said the woman.

"Yeah, okay, I'll stick to the deal," her partner groused, his expression looking as if he'd swallowed a lemon.

CHAPTER 18

When I woke up the next morning, I tried to remember my dream. Something about a baby crying, a loud wail that hurt my ears.

Then, in the distance, I heard the sound again – a siren. The police.

Jumping up, I raced to the window. Two police cars were pulling into the bookstore's sloping driveway. I'd been sold out.

Just then, the door opened and Estell motioned for me to follow. "Hurry, John, the police are here."

I grabbed my clothes and the go-bag, then followed her down the hallway to stairs that led up to the third floor. This upper level of the building was reserved as the owner's quarters. As far as I knew, nobody had ever been up there, other than Marlon and Estelle. They kept their home life private.

Their large living room was gorgeous. Wonderful antiques and original oil paintings adorned the space. I recognized a painting by James McNeill Whistler. It must have been worth a fortune. Marlon and Estelle must be rich. No wonder he was able to run this money-losing business. And he could afford to turn down my two hundred thousand, it appeared. So he had called the police.

"In here," said Estelle, opening a door that revealed a set of narrow stairs leading upward.

"I thought we were on the top floor."

"We are. This goes up to one of the gables. I'll move this oak armoire in front of the door so nobody will find you. Go up there and keep quiet."

~ ~ ~

Officer Ed Johnson was put out. "What do you mean he's not here?"

"Sorry, false alarm," said Marlon Klett, leaning on the counter with his elbows.

"That's right," echoed Estelle Bennington. "We saw a tramp coming this way from the back pasture and mistook him for John. Lots of tramps walk the old railroad tracks back there."

"Guess we jumped the gun, dialing 9-1-1," said Marlon. "We were just trying to be good citizens."

Officer Johnson shook his head irritably. "Well, you've wasted public resources, bringing us all way out here. Gas is expensive, you know."

Marlon shrugged. "What can we say other than *oops*?" The conversation was obviously over.

"Since we came all way out here, d'you mind if we look around, take a walk through the building?" said a second cop, Officer Reid Grandy according to his nametag.

"You got a search warrant?"

"Do we need one for a friendly look around?" replied Grandy.

"I guess not," acquiesced Marlon Klett. "Help yourself. But keep your hands off the books."

"That's okay," said Grandy. "I'm not much of a reader."

~ ~ ~

From the large gable window, I watched as the two police cars drove away, no lights or sirens with this exit. Somehow Marlon and Estelle had retracted their phone call reporting me. I had heard the police shuffling around on the floor below me, but no one found the stairs to the gable.

Now, there was a scraping sound as Marlon helped Estelle move the oak armoire aside, exposing the door to the stairs. I made my way down them, holding onto the railing because of the steepness. They were so narrow, my shoulders brushed the walls on either side. Apparently, Estelle had laundered my clothes overnight, and I didn't want to get my white shirt dirty. I'd always been a fastidious dresser, concerned about my looks. My wife and I had that in common.

"Looky who's been up in the gable," Marlon greeted me. "You're lucky that Ed Johnson didn't do a better job of searching the place. But he was bummed and ready to go back to the station."

"Thanks for hiding me," I said to Estelle. To Marlon, I said, "Thanks for turning me in. Your money's going back to my original offer, one hundred thousand."

"But you promised two."

"That was before you called the police on me."

Marlon tried to backtrack. "I didn't call the police. They were acting on an anonymous tip. Someone saw you climbing up them collapsed railroad tracks."

"Like who?"

Marlon shrugged. "Some passing motorist, they said. There would be a clear view from Deadman's Bend."

Estelle loyally didn't speak up, but from her expression she didn't like her partner's cover story. She may have even rolled her eyes. She was never one for lies.

"Give me another day or two, and I'll stick to the two hundred thousand," I told them. "But you better not call the cops again. They will be pissed off and so will I."

CHAPTER 19

When I got dressed and went downstairs the next morning, I could smell the coffee brewing in the corner of the main room. I made a beeline for it and poured myself a cup, taking it black today. I stuffed three glazed donuts in my mouth and gulped them down, hardly chewing.

"Hey, leave some for the paying customers," complained Marlon Klett from the counter. He was sorting the daily newspapers that had just been delivered.

There were no customers yet, but people would shortly be dropping by to pick up a paper. Home delivery was poor up here on the plateau, so most edge-of-towners got the *Daily Telegraph* from Klett's Bookstore. Marlon and Estelle did a pretty good business with newspapers, coffee, and fresh donuts. Estelle baked the donuts herself in the back kitchen.

I strolled over to the counter to check the headlines in the *Daily Telegraph*. Maybe it would have something about the investigation of Marilyn Zephyr's death.

It did.

The front page blared:

MURDER FUGITIVE STILL ON RUN.

The article identified me as the primary suspect, saying my fingerprints had been found at the scene. Of course they had, I told myself. My wife had been Marilyn's best friend. We went over there often, playing bridge. Iggy Walton had been the fourth partner. He had been seeing Marilyn since her husband died a few years ago.

Marilyn's husband's car had been hit by a semi that lost it brakes on the 102 hill into town. He had been squashed like a bug. The truck's driver had failed to use one of the run-offs. Marilyn got a big settlement from the trucking company. She had been sitting pretty – till someone blew her head off.

"What's it say?" inquired Marlon, taking the paper out of my hands, folding it, and replacing it on the stack with the others.

"Nothing new. They still haven't found Marilyn Zephyr's killer."

"That would be you," stated the bookstore owner. "You don't fool me."

"I told you I'm innocent. Someone mistook seeing me go into Marilyn's house. We live next door. The witness confused our house with hers."

"I'd stick to that story," advised Marlon. "It sounds plausible. When it comes to the trial, all you need to get off is reasonable doubt."

No way I could hide my frown. "There's not going to be a trial, at least not with me. I told you I'm innocent. Somebody else will be on trial. I'm sure mine weren't the only fingerprints found there. Iggy Walton's would be all over the place. He was practically living there. Slept over two or three nights a week. Hell, for all I know, Iggy could have killed her."

"Ignatius Walton is not a murderer. I went to school with him. He's afraid of guns. An old hunting accident turned him off of firearms. He wouldn't of shot her."

"How about me? I'm not exactly a gun nut. You won't find a single pistol or rifle in my house."

"Police will be checking with Bob's Pawn Shop & Gun Depot. He will know who owns guns around this town."

"Bob won't be much help. He distrusts the police." I wasn't sure whether my words were confidence or hopefulness.

"Sure he would. Yesterday's paper said Mrs. Zephyr was shot with a .32 caliber revolver. Bob will know who has a .32, who buys .32 ammo. He sells lots of bullets."

"Well, that will clear me. They can check Bob's records. I'm not a customer. I don't own a .32 Charter Arms Undercoverette snub-nose revolver."

Marlon Klett gave me a strange look, and I realized I'd said too much. Oh well, Marlon thought I was guilty anyway.

CHAPTER 20

Another day passed. The *Daily Telegraph* announced to its readers: **NO NEW BREAKS IN ZEPHYR MURDER.** I thought the heat might be dying down. Maybe I would slip into town to check on my wife. I wondered how she was taking all this. I was surprised she hadn't been quoted in the paper. Or made an appeal for me to turn myself in to the police. But she had been as silent as the grave. I wondered what she was up to. Probably letting me stew in my own juices.

"Marlon, can I borrow your car?"

"That'll be extra."

"What? You're charging me to use your car?"

"Hey, I'm not Hertz. I'd want another ten grand for a one-day rental."

"You're a crook."

"No, I'm a businessman. Someone has to profit from this mess you've got yourself into."

"Okay, ten. Give me the keys."

He reached into the drawer under the cash register to retrieve a jangly key ring. "Don't ride the brakes. I need new linings. Gotta take it over to Fast Moe's Mufflers and Brakes. They got a special on brakes. You get a free oil change with each brake job."

"Thanks. I'll be back this afternoon."

"How many more days you staying?"

"As many as it takes. There should be a break in the case soon."

"Are you going by the bank while you're out?"

"No, it's too soon. Besides, you don't get paid before this is over. Got to make sure you hold my room."

"Does this look like Holiday Inn? You can't stay here forever."

"For two hundred and ten grand, I expect a few more days without complaint."

"Where you going with my car? I don't want it to wind up like my old school bus."

"I just want to do a drive-by of my house, see if my wife's home."

"Your wife –?"

"What about her?"

"Nothing," he said. But I could see there was something he wasn't telling me.

~ ~ ~

Slowly, I drove past my house on Morning Glory Drive looking for any signs of my wife. I was nervous being in Marlon's beat-up canary-yellow Chevy Impala. The car stood out like a flag. The house looked empty. There was no sign of movement in the windows. The yellow police tape across the front door looked unbroken. I noticed that my Ford was missing from the driveway, but that probably meant the police had impounded it.

I wondered if my wife had taken refuge at her cousins' house, away from newspaper reporters and leering public. Maybe I'd find her there with Randy and Mitzi. But I couldn't remember their address. Somewhere "on the other side of town," she used to say.

Didn't she have an address book? I seemed to recall one in her desk drawer. Not that I'd been snooping. I was looking for postage stamps at the time.

Nothing else to do, I had to go inside the house and look for Randy and Mitzi's address. Maybe pick up my baseball bat. I had unfinished business with that woman.

I parked the '96 Chevy Impala on the next street over and entered my house through the backyard. We kept a spare key under the flowerpot. The house was quiet, my footsteps echoing on the wooden floor. "Honey, I'm home," I called out in my best Ricky Ricardo voice, but got no response. The house was empty.

I went upstairs to the bedroom to make sure my mind wasn't playing tricks. But it was just as neat as Mrs. Mueller had left it. Not a speck of blood or brain matter.

Searching my wife's desk didn't turn up her address book. There had to be some other way to find her cousins' address. Down in the kitchen I found a stack of unopened mail. I shuffled through it, thinking maybe she had a letter from them. Nothing but overdue electricity and water bills. They needed to be paid. My wife used to keep up with that stuff. I'd have to speak to her about it.

Then, I got an idea. About time the big inventor used his brain, I muttered to myself. There was a box of old Christmas card in the closet under the stairs. She sometimes saved envelopes for the return address on them, the beginning of a list for next year's SEASON'S GREETINGS.

Pulling out the dogeared cardboard box, I plowed through it, tossing Christmas cards and envelopes right and left as I checked them for any addresses. Here was my Aunt Freda's old address, but she'd been dead for ten years. And here was a card from Marilyn Zephyr next door. And there was a card from our insurance salesman. And one from Frederick Woolworth, my business partner.

Then *eureka*! An envelop with no name on the return address, but a street address – 253 Bluebird Lane – that I knew was on the other side of town. That had to be Randy and Mitzi's location. I could be there in twenty minutes, depending on traffic.

I was halfway out the door when I remember the baseball bat – a genuine Louisville Slugger. It was propped in the hall closet near the front door. Retracing my steps, I retrieved the wooden bat. My bat was made of maple but many are white ash. The name came from the nickname of legendary Louisville baseball player Pete Browning. According to the story, Browning broke his bat before a game and a man named John Hillerich made one for him out of maple. Turns out, maple is less likely to break than white ash. Hillerich went on to found a bat company in Louisville.

My thoughts were interrupted by the sound of a car pulling into the driveway. Through the peephole in the front door, I could see a police cruiser. Officer Johnson on the scene. I wondered if they had wired the place with an alarm that told them someone had entered the house.

Johnson was alone. He was heading toward the front door which meant no one would be covering the back. Dropping the bat, I raced down the hallway, through the kitchen, and into the mud room, where I threw open the back door and ran across the lawn toward the tall wooden fence.

Before I climbed over it, I peeked through a crack and spotted another police car in the back alley. Officer Grandy was headed my way.

Uh-oh.

Turning, I tripped over a garden hoe. The handle flew up and hit me in the face. My nose started to bleed, but I didn't have time to pull out a handkerchief.

"*Aoeeeee!*" I yelped.

My eyes were blurry and I thought I heard bells inside my head. The spot where I'd had my concussion began to ache.

Ka-bam! Ka-bam!

That noise, what was it?

When a bullet splintered through the wooden fence, I realized someone was shooting at me. Officer Grandy – the jerk was trying to kill me!

About then, I wished I still had that Charter Arms revolver. I had no way to protect myself. Grandy was shooting at an unarmed man. He hadn't even called for me to stop or to put my hands up.

Ka-bam!

The bullet barely missed me. I heard it whiz past my head like an angry hornet. There in the middle of my well-manicured lawn, I was an easy target. He was going to hit me sooner or later. He couldn't be that bad a shot.

Ka-bam!

Another problem, the shots would bring Officer Johnson on the run. He had a gun too. I would be caught in a crossfire.

But I wasn't ready to give up.

Ka-bam!

Keeping my head low, I veered to the left, hopping over the picket fence that separated our property from Marilyn Zephyr's. Landing in her rose garden, I almost yelled again when my skin met with the prickly stems of those American Beauties. My arm was scratched pretty badly, but I got up and ran around her house, crossing the street and making my way to where Marlon's yellow Chevy was parked.

Before you know it, I was on the Crosstown Boulevard. The town is divided into an X, with Crosstown going east and west, Main Street dissecting it north and south. Traffic was light and I carefully kept below the speed limit. I could be at Bluebird Lane before Johnson and Grandy finished searching my house. The dolts, they were like the leads in a Laurel and Hardy movie –but with Glock 19 semi-automatic pistols!

CHAPTER 21

Just when I thought things were going well, no cop cars following me, nobody shooting at me, I spotted a traffic stop up ahead. A police officer I didn't recognize was checking driver's licenses. There was obviously a bigger dragnet out for me than I'd realized. Our town didn't get many murders. This was likely the most excitement the local police had had in a dozen years.

I knew the police chief – Big Bill Dozier. I'd donated to the Police Little League Fund. But that wouldn't cut any ice with Big Bill. He was as hardnosed as a diamond drill. Before coming here, he'd been a cop in Chicago.

Nearing the traffic stop, I knew I had to do something quick. Seeing a sign that said PARK HERE- $3 PER HOUR, I made a hard right up the ramp into the five-story parking garage. The tallest building in town, it was higher than the building code allowed, but it was owned by the Mayor.

I selected an open spot on the third level, stuck the parking ticket under the visor where Marlon Klett could find it, and hoofed my way down the cement stairwell to the ground floor.

Now on the sidewalk, I had to figure out how I was getting to Bluebird Lane.

Ducking into an alley, I worked my way around the traffic stop that was blocking Crosstown Boulevard. Then I looked for a taxi.

There were two taxi companies in town – Convenient Cabs and Tom's Quick Taxi. Convenient was larger with about a dozen vehicles; Tom's had only two. You could tell the two companies apart by the color of their cabs. Convenient's were canary yellow; Tom's were robin's egg blue.

Luckily, I saw a blue cab heading my way, having cleared the traffic stop. The light on top indicated it was empty. The bad news was that owner Tom Pettigrew was driving. He was sure to recognize me. We saw each other once a month at Rotary Club meetings. We were both on the Membership Committee.

I turned to a boy walking down the sidewalk, a book bag slung haphazardly over his narrow shoulders. "Hey kid," I called to him. "I'll give you ten dollars for that baseball cap."

"No way," he replied, trying to ignore me.

But I stepped in front of him, blocking his path. "Fifty dollars," I said. "I like that cap." It was black with the high school baseball team's name emblazoned on it – the Tumbleweeds.

"Fifty bucks?"

"Right," I said, pulling five $10 bills out of my wallet. Looking over my shoulder I could see the approaching taxi. "But you've got two seconds to make up your mind or these sawbucks goes back in my wallet."

"I'll take it," the boy said, quickly handing me the cap.

He was still admiring his newly gained wealth when I stepped onto the steaming pavement of Crosstown Boulevard and raised my arm to hail the taxi. As it pulled up, I crammed the cap down on my head – a tight fit – pulling the bill down over my face. Climbing into the roomy backseat, I tossed my go-bag onto the seat next to me and muttered in a gruff voice, "253 Bluebird Lane."

"Want me to stay of Crosstown Boulevard or take the shortcut?"

"Shortcut sounds good," I mumbled.

"You got it, Chief," Tom Pettigrew said affably, making a left at the next corner.

I kept my head down as if I were reading the magazine I found in a pocket in the back of the passenger seat – a giveaway titled *Taxi Talk*. A plexiglass wall separated me and the driver, a barrier that allowed me to discourage conversation.

Tom was a good driver, knew the town well. Zigzagging among the side streets, he arrived at the destination sooner than I expected.

Cramming a $10 bill into the slot in the plexiglass, I muttered, "Keep the change." I exited cab, my head turned toward the house as if checking the address. I don't think he recognized me.

When Tom pulled away, I straightened up and marched to the front door. Next to the knob was one of those Ring doorbells that allows an owner to see who is at the door. I didn't want to announce my presence, so I stood so close to it the video camera could only pick up my belt buckle. Pressing the doorbell conjured up a disembodied voice asking who was there?

"Orkin," I said. "We're here for your roach inspection."

"We didn't order any roach inspection."

"It's complimentary. Your name was selected as this week's prizewinner by Shouting Sam, the DJ on the morning show at KLBM."

"Okay, just a minute. We listen to Shouting Sam all the time. But we didn't hear anything about a contest."

"Want the bug inspection or not?" I pressed.

"We'll take it," the voice confirmed. The door opened to reveal a teenage girl. Maybe 17 at most. This couldn't be right. My wife didn't have any teenybopper cousins that I knew about.

"Are you Mitzi?" I asked."

"Who?"

"You know, Mitzi and Randy."

"Oh," she said, disappointment filling her voice. She could see her radio prize disappearing. "You got the wrong address. We're 253 Bluebird Lane. You want 258."

I wasn't sure what to say, so I muttered a polite "Thank You" and walked five houses up the street. There it was – 258, the numbers posted on the side of a cinder-block cottage in large gold letters. I must have read the handwriting on the Christmas card wrong. It was easy enough to mistake a scribbled 3 for an 8.

The place was more rundown than the immaculate Tudor I'd just visited down the street. There was a large Harley-Davidson Fat Boy motorcycle propped on its kickstand in the driveway. The shrubbery needed watering. Weeds lined the slate walkway like miniature corn stalks.

This door had an old-fashioned button-style doorbell that played a chime version of "Zip-a-Dee-Doo-Dah," that passage about "Mr. Bluebird on My Shoulder." Uncle Remus sang that song in Disney's *Song of the South*, but the movie is politically incorrect today, a story of happy slaves working on the plantation. But I suppose if you live on Bluebird Lane it was okay to use it for your chimes.

When the door opened, I put my foot in the crack just for insurance. I wasn't sure whether or not my wife's cousins would be happy to see me, especially with that murder thing hanging over my head. Word was getting out.

The woman facing me had frizzy hair, like she'd stuck her finger into an electrical outlet. Her lipstick was on crooked. She bumped into a table near the door – what a klutz.

"Mitzi?" I said.

"Yes, can I help you?"

"I'm John, your cousin's husband. May I come in out of the sun?"

"Aren't you the one the police are looking for?"

"That's me. But it's all a mistake. I'm sure my wife can tell you that. Is she here?"

"Your wife – are you crazy?"

Ordinarily, I would have to consider that possibility, but today I didn't have the time. "I want to see my wife," I demanded angrily.

"Get your foot out of the door," she screamed, trying to shut the door.

"Let me come in," I insisted, keeping my foot in place. Unfortunately, I'd left the Louisville Slugger back at the house when the police showed up. Cousin Mitzi could use a good swift whack on the side of her head.

"Randy, come here quick," she shouted. "John's at the door. He's acting crazy."

A muscular man with a mohawk appeared behind her. He was wearing dark blue denim shorts and a green T-shirt that said, HELL'S WARRIORS in bold letters. His body was covered in tattoos. That explained the Harley in the driveway. He did not look like a man you'd want to tangle with. I removed my foot from the door and stepped back out of punching reach.

"Excuse me," I said meekly, "but I'm here to see my wife."

"Man O Man," exclaimed Randy, "you are a real wacko. Sorry about everything that's happened, but you gotta go. You're upsetting Mitzi."

"I didn't kill that woman," I said. But by then he had slammed the door in my face.

CHAPTER 22

Sometimes you just don't know what your next move should be. Randy and Mitzi were acting as gatekeepers to keep me from my wife. Maybe my wife was hiding from me on the theory "If you can't find me, you can't kill me." That was a problem.

Should I go see Bob at Bob's Pawn Shop & Gun Depot to buy another revolver, something bigger like a Colt Python 357 Magnum? This was a pistol that would put a hole in Randy as big as a fist. A 357 would even stop a bear.

But no, the police would have been all over Bob by now. His resolve to hide my identity may have weakened. He might even call the cops if I showed up. Or worse, shoot me with one of his AR-15s.

Where should I go to ground? I couldn't go back to Klett's without Marlon's car. That rusty old bus was one thing, but Marlon truly loved that '96 Chevy Impala. The car had sentimental value. Back when it was brand new, he'd pulled it into a Sonic where Estelle worked as a car hop. It had been love at first sight between the two. He took her for a ride in the big yellow Impala in leu of a tip. They never came back.

If not Klett's, then where?

I couldn't go back to my house. It appeared the police had it rigged with some kind of silent alarm. That would be like a roach marching into a Roach Motel. "Roaches check in, but they don't check out!" as the slogan goes.

Maybe I could hide out at the office. I'd slept on the couch in the lobby before. But no, Frederick Woolworth would turn me in. Underneath that slick salesman exterior, he was a civic-minded do-gooder. I'd recently learned that he serves on the Town Council. I wish I remembered more about him. There was undoubtedly some chink in his armor, but I didn't know enough about this stranger pretending to be my partner to ferret it out.

Maybe I could crash with Mitzi or Randy – the ones who worked at Wonder Works, not the gargantuan and his over-permed wife who were my wife's cousins – but I suspected that my Mitzi and Randy lived together, so that wouldn't work out.

My best friend was Jim Swanson, owner of Swanson's Construction Inc. But I wasn't sure how he'd feel about harboring a wanted criminal. Jim had been a policeman before starting his own construction company, and still had an affinity for the "boys in blue."

I paused to think about that. People always talk about the boys in blue, the blue flu, the blue wall of silence, the thin blue line. But the police in our town wore brown uniforms that made them look like Nazis without armbands.

My attention snapped back to the problem at hand when a man standing in front of a corner bodega said, "Say, don't I know you from somewhere?"

"Afraid not," I said, pulling my Tumbleweeds ball cap lower and increasing my pace. Whether he actually knew me or had simply seen my picture in the paper this morning didn't matter. Those two worlds were colliding. Anyone who recognized me would be calling the police to collect the $20,000 reward offered for information leading to my "arrest and conviction," so said a public service announcement that appeared in a box at the bottom of the *Daily Telegraph*'s front page this morning.

The man at the bodega kept staring at me until I turned the corner. I'd better hotfoot it, I told myself, before he placed where he'd seen me.

~ ~ ~

Skirting around the traffic stop by taking a side street, I found myself in a neighborhood I didn't recognize. I had gotten somewhat disoriented in my haste to put distance between me and the man at the bodega. This section of town was more run-down than, say, the Main Street area (which was known as The Marvelous Mile). This street could be called The Miserable Mile – although a sign on the corner identified it as Sunflower Avenue. It was lined with warehouses and abandoned buildings and cheap flop houses that often rented rooms by the hour. Hmm, maybe this was far enough off the beaten path that nobody would be looking for me here.

I thought about holding up in one of the abandoned buildings, but I quickly learned that this was the domain of drug addicts, alcoholics, and homeless zombies. They were not big on sharing their space. So switching gears, I presented myself at the front desk of a hostelry called The Palace Hotel, a misnomer so off the mark as to be laughable.

"Room?" the desk clerk greeted me.

"Do you have a monthly rate?"

"Dunno," he said. "Nobody's ever stayed a month before."

"I've got money," I said.

"Why do y' wanna stay here at The Palace?" the man asked suspiciously.

"I'm a writer," I improvised. "I'm looking for an out-of-the-way place where I can hole up and work on my book. It's about the homeless, so I thought this neighborhood would put me in the mood."

"It oughta do that all right," the desk clerk allowed. "What about eleven hundred a month? I could get more than that renting rooms out by the hour, but yours would be steady. For a month, I can give you what might be called a bulk rate discount."

"I'll take it," I said, peeling off the bills and laying them on the counter for him to re-count.

"Do you have any luggage?"

"Just this," I presented my go-bag.

"That don't hold much."

"I like to travel light."

The desk clerk was a thin-faced guy with gray hair and a pencil-thin moustache. He was in shirtsleeves due to the heat of the day. The Palace didn't offer air conditioning. "Call me Earl," he said. "I will be your host. I'm here 8 to 12. Harold handles the night shift. I should warn you, we have a fairly active night business, lots of coming and going. I hope you're a sound sleeper."

"I sleep like the dead," I assured him. "Nothing will bother me."

"D'you want a room on the first floor, second floor, or third floor? This time of day, lots of rooms are open."

"How about a corner room on the second floor?" I figured if I opened two corner windows I might pick up a breeze. Otherwise the place would be like a Navajo sweat lodge.

"Excellent choice. I'm gonna give you what we call the Presidential Suite."

"A suite?"

"Don't let the name fool you. It's only a single standard room, but the president of Sunrise Savings & Loan once had a tryst there. That's how it got its name."

~ ~ ~

The room was as expected, nothing to write home to mother about – even though there were complimentary packs of instant coffee and postcards on the desk. They showed a hand-colored photograph of The Palace Hotel in better days. Underneath it was the catchphrase, "Relax like a King." I wondered what king might have stayed here to give it that tagline.

That reminded me of the president of Sunrise Savings & Loan – a man named J. Jonathan Rollins. I knew him from the Rotary Club. I had to figure out how to withdraw some of my money deposited there. I was running low on pocket cash. And I owed Marlon Klett a bundle, two hundred and ten thousand dollars.

Perhaps I could get to the bank wearing a disguise. But I'd have to reveal myself to a teller to withdraw that much money. That would be a problem. Tellers are not well paid, and a $20,000 reward for my arrest and conviction would be very tempting, even for the most sympathetic bank clerk.

Foolishly, I was assuming that not everyone in town believed I was guilty. People generally liked me, as best I remembered. Sure, I have been a bit reclusive since that bomb accident. The concussion had put me in a coma for seven months. That takes you out of circulation. God only knew how many Rotary Club meetings I'd missed.

Maybe it would be simpler to rob the bank, I mused, only half-serious. Shucks, I couldn't even do that without a gun. My Charter Arms .32 was irretrievable, buried in three feet of cement. Bob was an untrustworthy gun dealer, as likely to sell out his own mother as not. Maybe – for a hefty price – Earl the deskman could procure me a gun off the street. But that might raise too many questions.

Looks like robbing a bank was not an option, I told myself as I lay on the lumpy bed. I was praying that the mattress wasn't infested with bedbugs.

Looking around the hotel room was enough to depress anybody. Peeling wallpaper, scarred wooden table, a toilet that looked like something had died in it, a sink stained orange with iron-rust.

The view out the window wasn't much better: An abandoned building with shadowy people coming and going, strange lights flickering in a third-floor window, rats as big as chihuahuas, and a broken water main that was spilling untold gallons into the street.

All the streetlights were broken, giving the place a dark and foreboding look. The potholes in the street could have swallowed a Volkswagen. Bricks falling from the building's façade were a danger to passersby, a sizeable pile of them currently blocking the sidewalk.

Things were seeming very dismal, until my thoughts turned to my wife. Sunrise Savings & Loan was a joint account. She could waltz in there and withdraw the money with a flick of a pen. But would she? After all, I'd been trying to kill her for the past year.

But I wasn't entirely sure my wife knew that. Somehow she had escaped every attempt, her attitude as oblivious as a show horse wearing blinders. Even if I could talk her into withdrawing the money, that would never happen if I couldn't locate her.

Where to look?

She wasn't home, that much was for certain.

I was halfway convinced she was hanging out with her lowlife cousins, Randy and Mitzi. But with that muscled biker standing guard duty, the chances of getting to her were about as good as being able to walk into the White House Oval Office unannounced.

To get inside that little cinder-block cottage on Bluebird Lane would take a tank. And where would I get a tank? The nearest National Guard armory was in the next town down 102. Forty miles away. Even if I could steal one, no way I could get it here without the entire United States military coming down on that slow-moving tortoise-like vehicle.

A bulldozer would be better. You could probably find one locally.

Then it occurred to me, my best friend Jim had one, a gigantic Caterpillar D11T CD. That sucker could move tons. It was the biggest crawler Caterpillar had ever manufactured. The pride of Swanson Construction. But how could I get him to loan it to me? And even if he did, could I figure out how to operate it? Just because I'm an inventor doesn't mean I know anything about heavy machinery.

But wait. I knew Jim did small jobs when they didn't interfere with his larger construction projects. He'd once told me he rented out his dozer complete with driver for $2,000 per day. Maybe we could do business.

CHAPTER 23

There was a house phone in the lobby of The Paradise Hotel that guests could use. "Just make sure it's a local call," Earl warned as he unlocked the cabinet that protected the phone from indiscriminate use. "And don't be on it all day. Some of the girls use it. Time is money for them."

"You got it," I nodded.

Fortunately, I knew the number for Swanson Construction by heart. It was actually Jim Swanson's cell phone. He ran his business on the fly. After ringing about 60 seconds, my friend answered. "Yo," he said. Not very professional, but he had plenty of business anyway.

Disguising my voice, I said, "Mr. Swanson, I have a quick demolition job. How soon could I rent your bulldozer and a trained operator?"

"We're not using the dozer right now, most of my men working on a house project over on Hollyhock Terrace. But I could peel off an operator and a driver to haul it to your site tomorrow morning at 9 a.m."

"That would work fine," I said in that gravelly voice. "I wouldn't need it for more than an hour or two."

"We charge by the day, whether you use it one hour or twelve hours. A flat fee of two thousand including delivery of the dozer. Does that work for you?"

"It does," I intoned. "Can I deliver the money to your man when he gets here in the morning. I'll pay in cash."

"That would work, Mr. –?"

"Hathaway. Jerome Hathaway. I want you to knock down the front of my rental property at 258 Bluebird Lane. I'm going to give the place a new façade."

"A new façade – we could bid on that too, Mr. Hathaway."

"Great. I will explain to your guy what I have in mind."

There was a pause. "We may have a slight problem," said Jim. "I didn't know you wanted to knock down part of a house. That will require some permits. No way we can get those approvals by tomorrow."

"Could we fudge a little? Do the job and follow up with paperwork later? Nobody at City Hall needs to know the order of things."

"Well –"

"I'll throw in an extra thou if you can get started at 9 a.m. tomorrow. I'm very eager to get this project going. Don't want to miss the Fall rental season. I'm going to turn it into an Air B&B. That's the way to go these days."

"An extra thousand, you say? And you'll have it all cash upfront tomorrow morning?'

"That's right. What do you say?"

"Okay, it's a deal. But you have to keep our delayed paperwork to yourself. The Building Department would have a cow if they knew. I could lose my contractor's license."

"Mum's the word," I said in my gravelly voice. "See your guy in the morning."

"258 Bluebird Lane, right? Wouldn't want to knock down the wrong house."

"Don't worry, I'll be there to meet your guy first thing in the morning."

~ ~ ~

Promptly at 9 a.m. I was waiting on the corner of Bluebird and Robin's Way, just down the block from my wife's cousins' house. I didn't want them to spot me. And this was a good vantage point to head off the truck bringing the bulldozer. A little stealth was called for with my plan.

From here, I could see the sidewalk in front of 258 Bluebird Lane. I wondered if my wife might walk out, but the only person to leave was Randy, his Harley roaring like an angry beast as he burnt rubber heading up Bluebird in the other direction from me. That was good, because now I wouldn't have to worry about him storming out with an AK-47 or some such when the bulldozer's wide blade hit the front of his house.

Th plan was to knock down the front door so I could run in and "rescue" my wife. No way were Randy and Mitzi going to lock her away from me. Those dorks!

I thought about letting the big Caterpillar kill my wife, knocking down the cinder-block structure on top of her. But

I needed her help in accessing my money at Sunrise Savings &
Loan. She could have her fatal rendezvous with destiny later.

I heard the grinding of truck gears coming up the hill. Just
because the town is in a valley didn't mean it was flat as a
pancake. The ground was wavy, with minor ups and down.
Bluebird Lane was on an upward slope, even though a slight
one.

Stepping out into the street, I waved the truck down. It
was a huge Peterbilt with a humongous yellow bulldozer sitting
on the truck bed. The driver leaned out the window and called,
"Mr. Hathaway?"

"That's me," I smiled. I hoped the driver didn't recognize
me from my visits with Jim at various construction sites. Even
if he did, he might not know my name. Jerome Hathaway was
as good a name as anything else for him.

"What are we taking down?" called the bulldozer operator,
sitting in the seat next to the driver.

"Just up the street there – 258. I just want to take down
the front wall, nothing else."

"You're paying us for a day just to do that?" said the
operator, raising his eyebrows. He had a squarish jaw with a
five o'clock shadow. He looked like he could be Italian.

"That's the deal."

"This'll take twenty-five minutes max, but it's your
money."

"Speaking of money, which one of you do I give this to." I
held up a fat envelope.

"Me," said the driver, taking it and stuffing it into the glove box. He was a swarthy guy with a slight accent. I couldn't place it. Maybe he was Italian too. We had a large community of Wops on the east side of town.

"Okay, go to it," I said, stepping back onto the sidewalk.

"Gotta unload this baby, then we'll be in business," said the driver. Just take a few minutes once we let the ramp down.

The operator had stepped out of the cab, and was surveying the house at a distance. "The dozer's almost too big for the job, that tiny little house. My blade's over 20 feet, almost as wide as the front of the house. Looks like it's cement blocks. They'll tumble down like a stack of children's ABC blocks."

"Yeah," said the driver. "This will take no time at all."

CHAPTER 24

The bulldozer lumbered forward like a prehistoric triceratops, its wide blade advancing toward the little cinder-block building like a predator about to strike. But the operator had a delicate hand. He moved the big machine into place carefully until the flat of the blade was barely touching the front of the house. The wide blade covered the screened door, the picture window, and what looked to be a bathroom window. Easing forward slowly, the façade tumbled inward with a loud *krack*! leaving behind a cloud of dust.

"What now?" he called down to me. "Want me to push the rubble into a pile?"

But no answer was forthcoming, for I had leaped past the blade into the now-open-to-the-outside living room. Looking around, I made sure there were no bodies among the cinder blocks. Then I stuck my head into the bathroom to make sure no one was trapped inside. Water was squirting from broken pipes, but the tiny room was empty.

Taking a deep breath, I stepped into the back bedroom where I encountered my wife's cousin Mitzi, sitting up in bed, wide-eyed with fear. "What's happening?" she asked nervously. "I was sleeping late … till the world came crashing down around me."

"Where's my wife?" I yelled, looking around frantically. But Mitzi was the only person in the room.

"Are you crazy?" she repeated her earlier accusation.

"Probably," I said, poking my hands into the clothes hanging in the closet, to make sure no one was hiding there.

"What's going on?" she repeated.

"Nothing. Just stay where you are."

"Where's Randy? He will handle this."

"Your hubby left on his motorcycle about an hour ago."

"He probably went to the diner for breakfast. Kerry's Korner Kitchen is just up the street. He'll be back soon. Then you can explain to him what's happening. He won't be happy."

Ignoring her, I ducked into the cubbyhole that served as a kitchenette. Nobody there.

The dozer had backed into the street, job done. Mitzi was out of bed, standing there in baggy pajamas, staring at the other side of the living room. The entire wall was missing, leaving only a pile of rubble along the line of the foundation. "Where's my wall?" she wailed, brushing the frizzy hair out of her eyes.

"Where's my wife?"

"You know," she shouted at me.

"Tell me or –"

"What the hell?" roared a bass voice. Randy had returned. His mohawk with standing up like the bristles on a brush. His tattoos seemed to dance on the surface of his skin. His muscles bulged like over-inflated balloons. He looked very intimidating.

"Hi Randy, I thought I'd drop by," I said.

"What's happening here? We don't own this place. We only rent. Is the owner demolishing the place without notifying us? We'll sue."

"Yeah, that's it," I tried to lead his thoughts away from me. A behemoth in size, he looked like he could break me in two like a matchstick. "Your landlord's kicking you out."

"Dammit, I shoulda paid the rent," he smacked his forehead as if suddenly understanding what had caused this disaster. "The landlord said he was gonna evict us. Guess this is how he's doing it."

"Have you seen my wife?"

He looked up, puzzled. "Of course I have. We're cousins."

"Who's the blood connection – you or your wife?'

"Mitzi is. Don't you see the resemblance."

"No," I said, looking past him at the woman with the bird's nest hair.

"They got the same bone structure."

"Yes, I think I can see that," Then an idea hit me like a pie in the face. "Tell you what, get your wife to run an errand for me and I'll send the bulldozer home."

His brow wrinkled, making the mohawk dance. "You can do that?"

"Absolutely," I said.

"What kinda errand?" he asked dubiously.

"Just have her go to the bank for me."

"Sure, that's not a big deal."

"She's got to pass herself off as my wife," I added.

"Now that *is* crazy," he said.

CHAPTER 25

Jim's bulldozer was gone. Neither the driver nor the dozer operator had recognized me as Jim's friend ... or as the wanted man featured in the *Daily Telegraph*.

As for Mitzi impersonating my wife, there were a number of things to consider:

- She had to avoid anyone who knew my wife, either personally or by sight.
- She had to know the details of the account, the ID number and all that. And have the bank book in hand.
- She had to look something like my wife, which meant getting rid of the hippie hair and hiding her tattoos.
- She had to be able to duplicate my wife's signature. That might be the biggest challenge. But chicken scratch was chicken scratch. It would just take practice.
- She had to have a good excuse for her actions if caught. Not that this was high on *my* list. But I didn't want the cops to break her and lure me into a trap when I met up with her to collect the money.

- Last thing, I needed some leverage to make sure she brought the money back to me, instead of skipping town with $300,000 in her suitcase.

Now could I get Mitzi to agree to this plan?

Randy was the key. He could just tell her to do it. She seemed fairly subservient to her brute of a husband. The question then, was how could I get ol' cousin Randy to go along?

~ ~ ~

"Randy, here's the deal," I said. "You've been kicked out of your home. Look at it over there, practically a pile of trash. Now, you and Mitzi need a new place to live. That takes money, but you don't have any."

"So?"

"I've got money. If you can get Mitzi to go to the bank and withdraw that money, I will give you fifty thousand dollars. Free and clear. You can get a nice place for that kind of money. First month, last month, damage deposit, even moving expenses would be covered."

"You'd do that for us?"

"Sure. After all, your wife is my wife's cousin."

"Her first cousin," he declared proudly.

"So do we have a deal?"

Randy nodded eagerly. "You bet, man. Just tell Mitzi what you want her t'do. She'll cooperate, I guarantee it."

~ ~ ~

That afternoon I'd given Randy some pocket money to rent a room in his name at Sunset Motel & Spa, a hostelry just five blocks away. That would give us a base of operations, much more comfortable than that shabby room at The Palace Hotel.

Room 307 was spacious, with a king-size bed and well-stocked minibar. It would serve nicely as a classroom, with me teaching Mitzi how to impersonate my wife. Too bad I didn't have the real deal, but nobody seemed to know where she was hiding. If Mitzi and her husband did, they weren't talking.

Turns out, Mitzi was a very good pupil. I found a canceled check in my wallet that had my wife's signature on it. All Mitzi had to do was duplicate the signature on a withdrawal slip at Sunrise Savings & Loan. That required practice, practice, practice.

She sat at the desk with a sheaf of paper, writing and rewriting the signature until it was practically second nature. I examined her work carefully: It might just pass.

While she worked on the signature, I'd sent Randy on his motorcycle to pick up some items from CVS. The list included Clairol hair color (an Auburn shade, like my wife's). Straightener. L'Oréal Paris lipstick (Rosy Red). Max Factor makeup. False eyelashes. My wife was a bit of a glamorpuss.

At Beth's Best Boutique, Randy picked up a simple black dress with long sleeves to hide Mitzi's tats. Also, he bought a pair of size 7 high heels. On his own, he bought a faux pearl necklace and matching earrings. Fancy, but my wife is fancy.

Now we were ready to transform Mitzi into my wife.

It was quite a makeover: First, Mitzi straightened her hair, ironing out the kinks. Then she dyed it, using Clairol Natural Instincts Hair Color in a shade called 30 Rosewood Dark Auburn Brown. Then she applied the Max Factor. And applied the Rosy Red lipstick, blotting her lips with a Kleenex. Fortunately, she had green eyes like my wife. The false eyelashes emphasized them beautifully.

Wiggling into the black dress, the transformation was complete. Mitzi was a caricature approximating my wife – straight red hair, elegant couture. She looked good in the black dress, her tats nowhere in sight. We added designer sunglasses to further mask her.

"Damn, you look good, babe," whistled Randy.

"I like this look," she winked. "I think I'm going to keep it. Goodbye, Motorcycle Mama! Hello, Femme Fatale!"

"Yeah. Maybe it's time we go more mainstream," agreed her husband. "I might even let my hair grow out."

She posed in front if the mirror, turning this way and that. "Hmm, I like being a redhead. I think my cousin was onto something."

"Works for me," he grinned.

"Let's hope it works for the bank," I said.

~ ~ ~

After another day's practice, it was time to rock 'n roll. We would call for a taxi to take Mitzi to Sunrise Savings & Loan on North Main Street. Randy would stay with me as a "hostage" to make sure she returned with the cash. That was iffy on several levels, but I was counting on her subservience to her husband to do as told.

"Your ride's here," I announced. Looking out the window as a blue Tom's Taxi pulled up in the parking lot. "Better get going."

"Okey-dokey," she gave a nervous smile.

"You've memorized my iPhone number, right? Call me if anything goes wrong."

CHAPTER 26

Mitzi stepped out of the taxi, and sauntered elegantly into the bank. My wife couldn't have made a better entrance. She headed to the teller at the far right. I'd warned her that the teller at the left window knew my wife. To withdraw $300,000 would require the approval of the President. But he didn't really know my wife, and I'd given Mitzi instructions on how to handle it if he balked at the withdrawal – which he undoubtedly would.

My fake wife smiled at the teller and slid the bank book across the marble counter. "Good morning," she said in a cultured voice. I'd given her elocution lessons best I could. "I wish to close out this account."

The teller looked at the bank book, eyes widening when she saw the amount. "Close it out? Is there some problem?"

"Not at all," the fake version of my wife purred. "I simply want to buy a Maserati. They are such wonderful automobiles, don't you think?"

"Uh, I wouldn't know. Excuse me for a moment. For a withdrawal this large, I need to get an officer's approval. Bank policy."

"Take your time," said Mitzi, as if she didn't have a care in the world. From what I've heard, she was mimicking my wife to a tee. Being a cousin, she'd had multiple occasions to observe her behavior.

The teller reappeared with the bank's president in tow. J. Jonathan Rollins was a portly man with an air of self-importance. "So good to see you again," he said, not realizing that he was speaking to an ersatz version of my wife. Mitzi was passing with flying colors.

"Yes, it's good to see you too," she faked it.

"What's this about closing out your account?"

"I plan to buy a new car – a Maserati GranCabrio Sport. They are a tad expensive, I'm afraid."

"Does your husband know you're doing this?" He was frowning, as if she were trying to wastefully spend the bank's own money.

"Oh yes. It's John's birthday present to me. He gave me the bank book and said I could buy any car I wanted up to three hundred thousand, the amount in this account."

"That's a very generous gift."

"Yes, isn't it. He's such a dear. His company – Wonder Works – sold a new product that has us rolling in money. He said to tell you he plans to come down and open a new account for this windfall. It will be at least seven figures."

"Oh my, that sounds wonderful," Rollins admitted.

"May I have my money? I'm in a bit of a rush."

"I'm afraid there are a few hurtles for such a large withdrawal. Forms to fill out, IRA reports to file, bringing in extra cash from other branches."

"Are you saying you don't have my money?" Mitzi shrieked, loud enough to catch the attention of other customers. Just like I'd coached her.

"Please, keep your voice down. This is a very delicate situation."

"Do you have the money or not?"

"Of course, we do, but a large withdrawal like this would deplete our reserves at this location. That's why this is managed at the corporate level."

"Are you saying that *you* don't have the authority to approve my withdrawal?" her voice shrieked again, drawing stares.

Rollins hastened to calm her down. "Yes, I have full authority. I am president of this branch."

"Well, give me my money. You can fill out the forms at your leisure. You have all the information about my husband and me on file."

"I'm sure we do, but I simply can't –"

"Poppycock. This is either our money or it isn't. If it is, give it to me right now."

"There's another matter. A cloud of suspicion hangs over your husband's head. I have to check whether the police have frozen this account or not."

"John was afraid you'd pull something like this, try to tie up our funds."

"You have to understand –"

"My husband said if you gave me any trouble to remind you of The Palace Hotel."

"The Palace Hotel?"

"Yes, The Palace Hotel."

"W-what are you talking about?"

"Don't play innocent. You remember that night about two years ago, that blonde hooker. I'm told there is security camera footage."

J. Jonathan Rollins turned pale. Leaning closer, he said: "Listen, you can't tell anybody about that. My wife would divorce me. I might lose my position here at Sunrise."

"Then give me my money and we will forget we ever had this conversation."

By now Rollins was cowed. He was breathing hard, as if about to suffer a heart attack. "Yes ma'am," he said meekly. "Your three hundred thousand will be out shortly."

CHAPTER 27

Randy and I were not at Sunset Motel when Mitzi returned by cab from the bank. As a precaution against her bringing the police, I'd moved him over to my room at The Palace Hotel. He was unimpressed with the new surroundings.

When Mitzi didn't find us at the Sunset Motel, she called the iPhone number I had made her memorize. "Where are you guys?" she demanded

"Never mind that. Do you have the money?"

"Yes, right here in a valise that J. Jonathan Rollins generously donated – three hundred thousand in crisp one hundred dollar bills. It's kinda hefty, about six or seven pounds."

"Did you run into any trouble?'

"None other than what you predicted with Rollins. I used your Palace Hotel zinger on him. He caved like a rotten tomato."

"Anybody with you?"

"You mean like the police? No, I told you there was no trouble."

"Call another taxi and come over to The Palace Hotel on Sunflower Avenue. Make sure you're not followed."

"There actually is a Palace Hotel?"

"Come find out."

~ ~ ~

Spreading the money on the dirty bedspread – three thousand $100 bills – I counted out $50,000 and handed it to Randy. "That's yours as promised. Make sure you spend it on a new place to live," I admonished. Nevertheless, I was pretty sure some of it would go for weed, Jim Beam, and a new Harley. Mitzi may have decided to pursue a new image, but Randy would have trouble changing his spots – or tattoos.

"Thanks, we'll do that," said Mitzi, taking the stack of $100 bills from her husband. Maybe her new persona had a backbone, I told myself. My wife certainly did.

Next, I counted out the $210,000 I owed Marlon Klett and put it in a neat stack. He didn't deserve it, trying to turn me in. I wondered if he'd found his Chevy Impala yet.

That left me with only $40,000. I needed it to replenish my working capital. Out of my $10,000 getaway money, I only had $1,525 remaining. Trying to kill my wife had been expensive.

~ ~ ~

"Now what?" asked Randy. His mohawk stood at attention, as if awaiting orders.

"I still need to find my wife."

"Look, man, you need help."

"That's what I'm doing – asking you for help."

Mitzi was silent. She looked really good with that red hair.

"Is there more money in this if we help you?" asked Randy. I could detect a touch of larceny in his voice.

"Ten grand if you lead me to her." Down to that last $40,000, I had to conserve my funds.

"That's gonna be hard t' do," he said, thinking it over.

"That's why I'm paying you ten instead of a thousand."

"We get the money if we lead you to her, no matter where she is?"

I wasn't following him. "Right," I confirmed the deal. "How long do you think it will take?"

"We know where t' find her. She ain't going nowhere. We can take you to her tomorrow."

"Good. Why don't you two go back to Sunset Motel. The room is paid through the week. I'll meet you there in the morning."

CHAPTER 28

Earl the desk clerk arranged for me to buy a car. I had abandoned Marlon's yellow Impala, and the police had impounded my faded-blue Taurus. I needed new transportation.

"There you are," said Earl with a flourish, indicating a candy-apple-red 2023 Dodge Charger parked at the curb in front of The Palace Hotel. "Just don't try to register it. And I'd avoid driving in the Evening Grove neighborhood. Somebody might recognize it, being red and all."

I handed him $10,000. My stash was dwindling. But I felt my quest was coming to an end. Randy was going to take me to my wife this morning. That would be another $10,000. After I paid off Marlon Klett, I'd be down to my last $20,000. Looks like I'd have to give myself a raise at Wonder Works.

Earl handed me the car keys. "Runs like a sonuvagun. Don't get caught speeding. State troopers go for red cars, y'know."

"Good advice," I nodded. The bright-red Charger was more gaudy than I was expecting, but beggars can't be choosers, as my mother used to say. I wondered whatever happened to my mother. I hadn't heard from her in years. My dad had died when I was 4.

Climbing behind the wheel, I fired up the Charger and listened to the 392 HEMI V8 engine's guttural roar. Standard on the Dodge Charger Scat Pack, the engine's naturally aspirated 485 horsepower and 475 pound-feet of torque can go from 0 - 60 in under 4.5 seconds. It was a genuine Hot Wheels.

I drove over to Sunset Motel to meet up with Randy. Knocking on the door, I heard a faint "Come in." When I stepped into the room, I had to catch my breath. There stood my wife, just like Randy had promised.

"Where have you been?" I asked.

She gave me a funny look. "What kind of question is that? Right here, of course."

"Sorry it has to end this way," I said, reaching into my go-bag and pulling out the Ka-Bar knife. This combat knife was adopted by the USMC in 1942 and has been standard issue ever since. It's known for its 7-inch carbon steel clip point blade and leather-washer handle. I bought mine years ago at Dusty's Army-Navy Store on South Main.

"What are you doing with that knife?" my wife asked in a quavering voice. I could tell she was scared. About time.

"All the better to gut you with," I replied.

"I'm getting out of here," she screamed, trying to run past me. I plunged the blade into her abdomen and that stopped her in her tracks. "Oh my," she said, looking down at the knife as if she couldn't believe this was happening.

I had trouble pulling the knife out; it seemed stuck. But I managed to extract it, then stabbed her again, this time in the heart. That's assuming she had one.

She staggered and fell down, blood seeping onto the carpet. Her auburn hair spread behind her head like a flaming pillow. "Nighty night," I said.

"You idiot," she uttered. "You got the wrong gal."

"I'll say," I agreed. "We were always a bad match."

She closed her eyes as if taking a nap.

Just then the door opened and Randy stepped into the room, carrying a six-pack of Bud Light and a bag of groceries. "What have you done?" he gasped.

"Killed my wife. Thanks for helping me find her."

"That's not your wife, you crazy fool. That's Mitzi."

I squinted down at the dead woman. "Are you sure?" I asked.

"She may look something like your wife – she decided to keep the red hair – but that's Mitzi. You've killed her."

If he was right, I'd made a bad mistake. But there were ways to fix this. I stepped outside onto the concrete balcony that ran the length of the building. Randy followed, towering over me like an enraged Sasquatch. "Let's talk about this," I cajoled. "What if I throw in an extra ten grand to make up for my mistake?"

"Mitzi ain't for sale."

Now that Mitzi was dead, Randy was going to be a problem. Looked like I'd have to get rid of him too. That was too bad, but I had little choice as I saw it.

Most people have heard of "cow tipping," that urban legend where college students tip over cows who "sleep" standing up. According to physicists, that's not easy. They estimate it would take at least 10 people to tip over a non-reacting cow.

Human Beings are easier.

While Randy yammered away, red faced and angry, I reached out with two fingers pressed against his breastbone and gave a little shove. He staggered backward, tipped over the balcony's wrought-iron railing and fell three floors to the ground. He landed in the asphalt parking space next to my new Dodge Charger with a *thud*!

Leaning forward to look over the edge of the balcony, I could see his hefty body down there on the pavement, a pool of red surrounding his head like a halo. "*Requiem æternam dona ei, Domine*," I said, making a sign of the cross.

I don't know why I did that; I'm not even Catholic.

CHAPTER 29

Now that I had cleaned up *that* mess, I needed to find a way to clear my name in Marilyn Zephyr's murder. According to the newspaper, her entire head had been blown off by a couple of .32 hollow-point bullets.

I gave the problem some thought. If I wasn't willing to be the fall guy, I had to come up with somebody else. The choice was easy – Marilyn's erstwhile boyfriend Iggy Walton. He had the means, motive, and opportunity, or at least would appear to after I finished.

Means? Iggy was a well-known gun nut. He must own twenty or thirty firearms. He used to brag about them while we played bridge. One of them was surely a .32 revolver.

Motive? A lover's quarrel. Happens all the time.

Opportunity? He had unfettered access to her house. Slept over. Came and went as he pleased. His fingerprints would be all over the place.

Now, I had to turn the cop's attention in ol' Iggy's direction.

That was easy.

~ ~ ~

Stopping by Wonder Works that night when nobody was there, I quietly let myself into my office and pulled my trusty old Smith-Corona out of the storage closet. Although the portable typewriter had long-ago been replaced by a PC computer, I just couldn't bring myself to throw it away. But now I would have to.

Placing the Smith-Corona on my desk, I pecked out a suicide note:

> I cannot live with myself after what I did to Marilyn. It is eating at my soul. I didn't mean to kill her. It happened in a moment of extreme emotion. I was cleaning my Charter Arms Undercoverette Model 73220 when we got into an argument over my moving in with her. I don't know what came over me. May God forgive me. Goodbye to all.
> Very truly yours,
> Ignatius Emmanuel Walton

Then I drove over to the old abandoned Finch farmhouse off Highway 83 and tossed my beloved Smith-Corona into the well.

~ ~ ~

Next I dropped by Iggy Walton's small house on Fairweather Avenue. That's on the southside of town. Retired from his job at Treadworthy Tires, I knew he was likely to be home. He seemed surprised to see me, but pumped my hand vigorously and invited me inside.

I muttered words of condolence, and gave him some lie about the police having cleared me in his girlfriend's death.

"I knew you didn't kill Marilyn," he said. "You and your wife were her best friends. We all played bridge together."

"All for one and one for all," I quoted Alexander Dumas.

"Exactly," he said, settling into a chair.

That's when I pulled the nylon cord from my go-bag and strangled him.

I know I said I didn't like physical confrontations, but you do what you gotta do. Iggy was a small man and didn't put up much of a struggle. It was over in ten minutes.

Laying out the typed suicide note on his kitchen table, I anchored it in place with a salt shaker. Then the thought hit me: Nobody commits suicide by garroting himself. It just wasn't plausible.

That gave me pause.

However, a solution came to me and I dragged his body into the garage, tied one end of the nylon cord around his neck and threw the other over a beam, hoisting him up like a side of beef in a meat locker. I placed a stool under his feet, then tipped it over as if he'd kicked it from under himself.

Done.

Iggy Walton had hanged himself out of remorse.

CHAPTER 30

I parked the red Charger in the lot outside Klett's Bookstore and ambled inside. Marlon Klett and Estelle Bennington were standing behind the counter sorting new books – titles by Patterson and King and Grisham. Local readers like pop literature.

"W-what are you doing here?" blurted Marlon.

"Have some business to take care of with you."

"Did you come to kill us?"

"Why would I do that?"

"Because I called the police on you."

"Water under the bridge," I dismissed his fears. "I'm here to pay you the money I owe you."

"You are?"

"Of course." I started counting out $100 bills on the counter. "There you go, two hundred and fifty thousand dollars. Paid in full. Enjoy the Grand Canyon."

"Have the police cleared you?"

"Not yet. But they will."

"Do you need your room back?" asked Estelle. "I put fresh sheets on the bed this morning."

"Maybe for a night or two, if you don't mind."

"Not at all," said Marlon, eyeing the stack of money. "We're happy to accommodate. We've always believed in your innocence."

"Thanks." Two liars, he was being untruthful about believing in my innocence and I was prevaricating about being thankful.

"I'm fixing pot roast for dinner," said Estelle. "And coconut cake for desert."

~ ~ ~

As I stretched out on the bed – it was far less lumpy than my mattress at The Palace Hotel – and thought over the events that had started with my concussion from that bomb. The experimental explosion-proof suit had simply been a scheme to blow up my wife. But somehow she had escaped the blast.

And she'd dodged all my other attempts to kill her. How did she do it? The woman was practically preternatural.

After all my efforts, she was still out there some place, probably laughing her ass off at my Keystone Kops antics. Should I just give up and file for a divorce? Never mind that $2-million life insurance policy I had on her.

No, I told myself. This had become a battle of wills. I'd be damned if I let her outsmart me. And what's to say that she might have her own little revenge scenario. My wife was devious.

She may well be plotting to kill me. Death by Cop had almost worked.

~ ~ ~

The next morning I skipped down the stairs, heading straight for the big coffee urn and the plate of donuts. Estelle had provided maple donuts with sprinkles, a major departure from the usual glazed variety.

Marlon didn't even complain when I took three.

"Help yourself," Estelle assured me. "I've got more in the kitchen."

"Seen the morning paper?" Marlon asked, waving a copy of the *Daily Telegraph* at me. "I think you'll find it interesting."

I took the proffered newspaper and examined the front page. The big headline above the fold proclaimed:

**ZEPHYR MURDER SOLVED –
LOCAL MAN CONFESSES.**

The lead told about the discovery of Ignatius Walton's body hanging in his garage. And that a suicide note placed him as the killer of Marilyn Zephyr, his sometimes girlfriend.

A few paragraphs down were a couple of throwaway lines to affect that all charges against me had been dropped and Police Chief William Howard Dozier was asking that I come in voluntarily to take care of some paperwork and receive his profound apologies.

That was another way of Big Bill Dozier saying he hoped I wouldn't sue.

At the bottom of the front page I noticed a smaller headline that said:

MURDER-SUICIDE AT SUNSET MOTEL.

That had gone well. "My nightmare is over," I sighed.

CHAPTER 31

Now that I was officially cleared of all charges and no longer the subject of a massive manhunt, I decided it was time to go home. Thanking Marlon and Estelle for their hospitality, I fired up the Dodge Charger and headed toward my house on Morning Glory Drive.

Making my way carefully around Deadman's Bend, I eased the Charger down the steep slope into town. Parking in my driveway, I climbed out of the car and waved cheerily to my neighbor across the street, the one who had fingered me as Marilyn Zephyr's murderer. "Nice day," I shouted.

I'm a forgiving kind of guy.

Surveying the front of my Georgian home, I noted that all the yellow crime scene tape had been removed. My wife's marigolds lined the front of the house with a brilliant array of yellows and golds and oranges and reds. The grass had been cut, a sign that my truckload of Mexican yardmen had been there.

The Zephyr house next door looked back to normal. You would never know it had been the scene of a recent crime. The roses in the garden were blooming, the petals as red as the blood that had covered the floor in the upstairs bedroom a few short weeks ago. The only thing that looked out of place was a big FOR SALE sign in the yard.

Practically dancing up the stone steps, I inserted my key in the lock – but to my surprise the door was ajar. Gingerly, I pushed it open and stepped inside.

"Dear, you're home," came a familiar voice.

I looked up to see my wife framed in the living room doorway, dressed to the nines like a cover photograph from a recent issue of *Vogue*. Her auburn hair was piled atop her head in a style reminiscent of Audrey Hepburn in *Breakfast at Tiffany's*. Yes, she looked *très* elegant as usual.

"Oh, hi," I replied, choosing my words carefully. For all I knew, she might have a 9mm Beretta hidden behind her back. "I wasn't expecting you to be here."

"Why ever not? This is our home."

"Yes, yes, of course."

"I'm so glad the police cleared you. Now we can get on with all our plans."

"What plans?"

"You know, going to Pamplona to see the Running of the Bulls. Taking a cruise to see the turtles at the Galápagos Islands. Feeding the sacred deer in Kyoto. Watching the Northern Lights play across the sky in Reykjavík. Snorkeling the Great Barrier Reef. All those things we talked about doing."

I didn't remember talking about any of this. "How about visiting the Grand Canyon," I said, referencing Marlon and

Estelle's Dream Trip.

"Oh, John. You're so silly. That's one of the things I love about you."

Love? Who was this doppelgänger? Was this the new Mitzi? Had I killed the wrong woman? Or not killed the right woman, to be more precise?

I blurted, "You know I've been trying to kill you, don't you?"

"Why would you want to do something like that?"

"Well, you know. Things haven't been going all that well between us."

"What does that matter now?"

I wasn't sure what she was trying to say. "Look, let's talk about this later. I'm tired. I've been on the run for a couple of weeks. It's a bit of a strain when everybody's trying to kill you."

"Yes, dear. I know what you mean."

~ ~ ~

I lay on the king-sized bed, the covers still on, my eyes closed. My wife snuggled beside me. But I couldn't get any rest. What if she tried to kill me in my sleep?

Maybe she had the same thoughts. I could sense that she was awake too.

Finally, I got up, saying I wanted a drink. "Would you like one too?"

She sat up in bed, still dressed in that black form-fitting sheath by Vera Wang. Not a knock-off like Randy had picked up for Mitzi at Beth's Best Boutique. "I'd love a mojito," she smiled, her lips that Rosy Red shade she always wore.

"Coming right up."

I made my way down the stairs toward the liquor cabinet in the living room. I was thinking about having a Johnny Walker Black. There was an unopened bottle in the back of one of the shelves as I recalled.

As I turned into the hallway, I noticed my go-bag lying on the floor near the front door where I'd dropped it when I'd been surprised by my wife's unexpected appearance. Walking over, I snatched up the bag and carried it to the liquor cabinet with me. Something about it was tugging at the back of my mind.

When mixing the mojito, grinding the mint leaves with a blunt wooden muddler, it came back to me. Opening the go-bag, I fished around till I found the toilet-paper-wrapped *Amanita phalloides*. The cap was large and plump, not as dried out as I expected after a couple of weeks bouncing around in the canvas backpack. Breaking off chunks into the mojito glass, I pulverized it against the mint with the muddler.

Ten minutes later, I was clinking glasses with my wife, saying *salut*!

"Hmm, this is good," she said, sipping mightily on the mojito, the meaty flavor of the mushroom hidden by the fizzy mint lime taste of the drink.

"Drink up," I encouraged. Thinking: "Success at last."

I waited the rest of the day and all night after that for her to start complaining of stomach pains or nausea – but *nada*. Ingesting one death cap mushroom is enough to kill a healthy adult. Why wasn't she showing any symptoms? This woman was indestructible.

~ ~ ~

In the morning I fixed us toast and coffee. The newspaper lay open-faced on the breakfast table for my wife to see. Its top-of-fold headline announced:

INVENTOR CLEARED
IN ZEPHER MURDER

A phone call yesterday afternoon to the editor-in-chief of the *Daily Telegram* had resulted in this major retraction. When I had explained that I was going to file a $2-million defamation lawsuit against the paper, he had seen the light.

"See, I told you everything was going to work out," she patted my arm.

"Thanks."

"Don't worry, I still love you even if you did kill my friend Marilyn."

"How do you know that?"

"Dear, I *am* your wife."

Pulling on my JoS. A. Bank suitcoat, I said, "See you tonight. I may be late. I'm going to need to catch up at work. Wonder Works has been chugging along without me for nearly two weeks."

"Have a good day," she winked. "I'll be waiting."

I wondered what she meant by that wink.

CHAPTER 32

Frederick Woolworth was surprised to see me show up for work. "My god, man, is it safe for you to be here? The police have been all over us for the past two weeks. We could hardly get any work done."

"Didn't you see today's paper? I've been exonerated."

"Yes but –"

"What have you guys been working on," I cut him off.

"Why, that Easy Bake Oven you came up with just before you disappeared." He gestured toward the Project Room. "It's coming along really well."

I didn't remember inventing an oven, easy bake or otherwise. But I didn't bother saying anything. I'd been pretty confused lately. "What's the principle? Switch on a 40-watt light bulb and wait two hours?"

"Very funny. I remember those working toy ovens by Kenner too. They used a pair of ordinary incandescent light bulbs as a heat source. Now they are made by Hasbro using real heating units."

"You seem to be up on toy kitchen appliances."

"Our oven is for adults, but I looked into the kids versions for copyright and trademark reasons. We can't use the 'Easy Bake' name other than as an internal product code."

"Too bad. But we will come up with something. How about Simple Bake?"

"I like that," he smiled. "John, you've still got it."

"Now, about the principle behind our oven –?"

"You oughta know, you clever rascal. Friction by subatomic particles is a totally new concept. Real Buck Rogers stuff."

"Right," I said, as if I had a clue what he was talking about.

"The cool thing is that it works without electricity. The subatomic fractionator is self-contained. People are going to love that. It will cut their electricity bills."

"I'd think so."

"Do you want to see the working prototype?"

"Not right now. I'll need to ease back into things. The past two weeks were quite exhausting."

"I can imagine, on the run from the law. I'm surprise Big Bill Dozier didn't order his men to shoot to kill. He was very agitated about your disappearance."

"They tried."

"No kidding?"

"I'm sure they will tell the story differently."

"Well, it's good to have you back at work. Some of those old ideas we recycled are starting to sale. Cash flow is looking up. And that Easy Bake Oven proves you've still got that old magic."

Try as I could, I didn't remember anything about inventing an Easy Bake Oven. I wondered if Woolworth was gaslighting me too?

"How are Randy and Mitzi doing?"

"Who?"

"You know, our staff."

"Oh, you mean Sandy and Martha. They got engaged while you were gone."

"I thought Randy was gay."

"Whatever would give you that impression? Those lovebirds have been living together for the past four years."

"They've worked for us that long?"

"You bet. Our employees are very loyal."

"Employees – there are only two of them."

"Yes, but they are very loyal."

"And their names are Sandy and Martha?"

"Old boy, I'm worried about you. Your brain seems a bit scrambled ever since that concussion."

"Yeah, it's been tough. Thanks for your concern, Fred."

"Ted. My name is Ted."

"Sorry, I meant Ted," I replied, playing along.

"Maybe you should consider cutting back your hours. Get a little rest."

I couldn't help but laugh. "I think I've used up my vacation time. I just took two weeks off."

"Well, give it some thought. Try working at home. Just feed us some ideas occasionally and we can take it from there. Sandy's getting pretty good at doing the heavy lifting."

"Sure, whatever you say."

~ ~ ~

Sitting in my office, I thought about it all: I was sure Sandy and Martha had been Randy and Mitzi. But so had my wife's (late) cousins. And so were my two (missing) children.

Was Frederick Woolworth (now known as Ted) trying to confuse me about the staff? If so, they had to have been in on it too.

Only my wife's cousins seemed real. But rather than the cultured pair she had painted them to be, they turned out to be a couple of lowlifes. And now they were dead.

Yes, I had killed the "real" Mitzi, mistaking her for my redheaded wife. Too bad, but what's done is done.

Everybody seemed to be playing with my mind lately. Was Frederick Woolworth somehow in cahoots with my wife to drive me crazy? For what reason? Were they carrying on behind my back? As I recalled, Fred had a perfectly good wife at home, although I didn't remember ever meeting her. But then my memory had been sketchy ever since that concussion.

Why was I trying to kill my wife? Truth is, I couldn't remember that detail either. It was just a compulsive drive, as unarticulated as a madman's incoherent ravings. There had to be a reason, but somehow I had forgotten it.

I was beginning to think I'd killed my neighbor too, mistaking Marilyn Zephyr for my wife.

Also, add to the list my murder of that poor schmuck Iggy Walton. He had done nothing to deserve his death other than play bad bridge hands when we were paired together. But he had provided a convenient solution to my problems. No reason I should pay for "accidentally" killing his girlfriend, right?

My mind was like a Vitamix blender. Everything was jumbled together. Maybe I should see a shrink. Or talk to a priest. Or get myself a lobotomy.

JFK's sister got a lobotomy and she never had to worry again. That might just make the painful procedure worth it.

The more I thought about it, I wondered if maybe I'd already had a lobotomy, somebody rummaging around in my brain with a leucotome, destroying brain cells, severing the connections in my prefrontal cortex between the frontal lobe and the thalamus, altering the way I thought and acted. That might explain my aberrant behavior.

Or maybe my aberrant behavior came first, and the lobotomy was a corrective measure that had only partially worked.

Gently probing my scalp with my fingers, I found the tender spot where I had suffered a concussion. A Humpty Dumpty head, my wife had called it – a cute name for my condition.

But maybe that wasn't it at all. Maybe this was the spot where a prefrontal lobotomy took place. That kind of procedure required a piece of the skull to be removed or drilled into. Had someone run a neurosurgical drill through my cranium while I was in that coma?

~ ~ ~

Wandering into the Project Room, I asked Sandy/Randy how the Easy Bake Oven was coming?

"Pretty good," he replied. "Want to see a demonstration?"

"No thanks. I'm more interested in how the gizmo works."

"You oughta know. It's your invention."

"Humor me."

"Producing heat from friction by subatomic particles, that was brilliant. I've got to hand it to you."

"I'm sure you added a few tweaks."

"A few," he smiled modestly. "You original concept was good, but had some bugs in it."

"Can you explain how you made it work?"

"Happy to," said Sandy/Randy. With no further encouragement, he began to ramble on, tossing around scientific terms and quantum theory. By the time he finished I was totally confused. Could I have possibly come up with this idea? I barely understood what he was talking about.

Noticing a squarish device covered with wires and switches sitting on a worktable in the corner, I casually asked, "Is this a part of the oven?"

"Don't touch that!" he yelped. Then he took a deep breath and said more calmly, "That's a bomb."

"Why would we have a bomb?"

"We're planning to retest your Explosive Ordinance Disposal suit. Last time you tried it was a disaster. I've made a few tinkers that might prevent the wearer from getting a concussion."

"Isn't it dangerous to leave a bomb sitting here on a table?" My words sounded scolding.

"We don't have much storage here, as you know. All the closets are full. And we don't have any containers that are bomb proof. So I've been keeping an eye on it till we can do the test."

"When's it scheduled?"

"Next week. We've got the Town Council's permission to conduct a controlled explosion at the old airport grounds. The fire department and paramedics will be standing by."

"Who will be wearing the Iron Man suit?"

"Me," he said. "Mr. Woolworth refuses to do it. And you've been out of condition."

"I'm feeling much better."

"The doctors would never let you do that test. You're still recovering from that concussion from the first time."

"Are you sure you want to be the one to wear the suit? You don't want to wind up like me. It sure scrambled my brain. I haven't been able to think straight since that day."

"Don't worry about that too much," he said. "You were always the Mad Scientist type."

CHAPTER 33

After lunch, I drove down to the police station and asked to see the chief. The rank and file clustered into the lobby to get a firsthand look at the guy they had been searching for the past two weeks. I wasn't sure whether they were friendly or not. I remembered Officer Grandy trying to shoot me in my backyard. I hoped there were no other zealots on the force. These cops were all carrying guns.

Big Bill Dozier came striding out like the cock of the walk. As his nickname implied, he was a big man, easily 6-foot-4 or -5 and a good 300 pounds. He was wearing a brown suit topped by a wide-brimmed cowboy hat. I could see a pistol poking out from under his suitcoat.

"I've come to turn myself in," I announced loudly to the assembled audience. I kept my hands visible, held out from my body as if I was preparing to fly into the air.

"What a joker you are," boomed Big Bill, grabbing my hand and shaking it vigorously. "We're honored by your visit."

"Well, uh –"

Big Bill plowed on: "We want to thank you for allowing us to use you as a diversion, while we were doing that hard cop work it took to identify the real killer."

What work did they do? I asked myself. I strangled Iggy Walton and provided a phony confession. All the cops had to do was answer the 9-1-1 call when a neighbor stumbled across Iggy's body.

The way he told it made it sound like I'd been working in concert with the police, practically an undercover agent helping them flush out the real killer. A complete fabrication, but I wasn't going to deny it. I needed all the help I could get in rehabilitating my reputation in this town.

"I congratulate all of you fine policemen for solving the crime," I said in a pseudo show of modesty. "I'm sorry for any problems I may have caused."

"You gave us a merry chase," Big Bill admitted. "But it worked to our advantage." A few newsmen had joined the crowd, so the politician in him was coming out.

The way he told the story, it was his brilliant plan to let me play fugitive to trick the murderer into letting his guard down. He yammered on and on, preforming for the three or four reporters who had shown up for my reappearance after two weeks on the lam. I got the impression they really wanted to talk with me, rather than the bloviating police chief.

Big Bill produced a few forms for me to sign – I didn't even bother reading them – pronounced me no longer a Person of Interest, and shook my hand again.

I said, "Am I free to go?"

"Of course, of course. But drop by and see us anytime. I would love to hear more about how you managed to elude us for so long."

I gave him a wink. "I'm like a magician. I never reveal how the trick was done."

~ ~ ~

On my way out the door, Officer Reid Grandy sidled up beside me and whispered, "You don't fool me, boy-o. You strangled Iggy Walton and I'm going to nail you for it. He was a buddy of mine."

I was taken aback. "What makes you say that?" I gulped.

"There was a typed suicide note, but Iggy didn't have a typewriter. We searched the house top to bottom."

"Maybe you didn't look hard enough."

"Don't get smart with me. I'm going to nail you for Marilyn Zephyr's death too. If Iggy didn't do it, that leaves you. That witness still sticks by her story."

Officer Johnson had joined us. Double teaming me. "That ain't all," he added. "The bomb that put you in the hospital, it went down as accidental. But we know you deliberately killed your wife. We just can't prove it."

"W-what?"

"You heard me," he said and moved away.

Officer Grandy gave me a knowing wink and followed his partner, a smirk on his face. Their gait had a swagger of satisfaction in it, knowing they had succeeded in intimidating me.

I stood there watching them go. My mind was racing, trying to understand what the two policemen had just said. Killed Iggy and his girlfriend – yeah, I did it. But my wife? That didn't make sense. She was at home waiting for me.

Noticing I was still standing there, Big Bill walked over and slapped me on the back. "Hey, if you like it here so much, I'll get a cell for you," he joked. "Go on home before I get out my cuffs."

Following his advice, I made my way down the front steps of the station, moving like a sleepwalker. What was that all about? Were Officers Johnson and Grandy just trying to rattle me? Was it sour grapes because I'd made them look bad, hiding at Klett's Bookstore under their very noses?

At any rate, they couldn't prove anything, else they wouldn't have allowed me to walk out of the police station. "Screw them," I muttered to myself, crawling into the candy-apple-red Dodge Charger. I was going home to see my wife.

~ ~ ~

Several cops were staring at my car as I drove off. That made me a little nervous. I was undoubtedly riding around in a stolen vehicle with phony plates. And being bright red, with a loud muffler and roaring engine, everybody noticed it. Had I been a fool, parking the car in front of a police station where dozens of cops were milling about? One of them had probably taken the stolen car report for a flashy 2023 Dodge Charger.

All the way to Morning Glory Drive, I made sure to keep my speed under 20 MPH. It was hard to hold back the 6.4-liter, 485-hp V-8 engine, like forcing a Preakness race horse to merely walk around the track. But having no registration, I couldn't afford to get stopped for a ticket.

My concerns about the policemen's comments faded when I stepped into the living room. My wife was lounging on the Onyx Sofa by Peugeot. She was wearing a translucent lace nightgown that emphasized her curves. I could see flashes of creamy white skin. Her auburn hair was down, flowing over her shoulders like lava.

"I've been waiting for you," she purred. "How did it go?"

"I'm a free man. All is forgiven," I replied. "You would have thought Big Bill Dozier was my best friend in the whole wide world."

"Speaking of best friends, Jim Swanson has to break up the foundation he poured for that spec house over on Hollyhock Terrace. It was too close to the property line. His crew will probably find that Charter Arms .32 snub-nose when they chip it out."

"How do you know this?" It wasn't clear whether I was asking her how she knew about this problem with the Hollyhock house ... or about the Charter Arms Undercoverette?

"You would be surprised what I know."

"You're not going to believe this, but a cop said I killed you."

"Which time?" she laughed as if hearing a funny joke.

"You know I'm going to."

"*Pish*! Come over here to the couch. You can always kill me later."

CHAPTER 34

"What are you and Frederick Woolworth up to?" I casually asked over breakfast. I'd scrambled some eggs, buttered the toast, and brewed coffee. My wife sat across the table, still rubbing sleep out of her eyes. She looked good even without makeup.

"I don't know what you mean. I barely know your partner."

"Neither do I. But I think you and he have been playing mind games with me. Taking advantage of my confusion following my seven months in a coma."

"I was very distraught when you were in the hospital."

"That doesn't answer my question."

"Freddie and I were merely friends. We saw each other socially a few times. But you already know that."

"I do?"

"Of course. Wasn't that why you set off the bomb? You've always been so jealous."

"It's coming back to me now. You and my business partner were having an affair. That's why I tried to kill you with the bomb."

"Tried? You did, dear. That's why I'm haunting you."

"You're saying that you're … dead?"

"You were there. You were wearing that stupid metal suit. Then you set off the bomb. All that was left of me was a pile of bloody rags and smoking chunks of meat."

"But I've seen you a zillion times since I came out of that coma."

"You did? Not really. I don't exist except inside your mind."

"You mean you're a figment of my guilty conscience?"

"You don't feel guilty. You're a social psychopath. I think the lobotomy removed the part of your brain that feels remorse."

"I had a lobotomy? I thought doctors didn't do that anymore."

"Sometimes they do. It's still legal. But obviously it didn't do any good. Just left you fixated on killing me. Apparently the de-braining made you forget you'd already done that."

"So you're dead? That's why I could never kill you, no matter what I tried?"

"You can't kill someone who's already dead," she shrugged daintily.

My blood pressure was rising. "I should have killed Frederick Woolworth too."

"You have a point there. It's not fair that he gets to run around alive, trying to get you declared *non compos mentis* so he can take over the business, while I'm condemned to be here with you."

"How do I get rid of you?"

"I have no idea. Obviously, killing me doesn't work the second time around."

"Or the third, fourth, and fifth."

"Believe me, I don't want to be here either. I'm still angry over being blown to smithereens by your stupid bomb."

"So all those confusing things you did, the gaslighting, that was for revenge?"

"Aw, I was just messing with you. Freddie is the one with an agenda. You never should have signed that partnership agreement with the 'survivor takes all' addendum."

"How did I get a lobotomy? You were already dead when I was there in the hospital. I have no living relatives. There was no one to sign for it."

"That was Freddie's doing. That *non compos mentis* thing he was trying to arrange. He provided the doctors with a phony Living Will that gave them all kinds of instructions for keeping you alive."

"You had me fooled. I thought you were still alive and dodging my attempts to do you in. You certainly look real."

"Thank you. I will take that as a compliment." She fluffed at her red hair as if primping.

"Could anyone else see you?"

"Of course not. I exist only in your enfeebled little mind. You've never seen me interact with other people. They don't know I'm there."

"What about the kids – Little Randy and Mitzi?"

"They weren't real. One of the neat things about being dead is all the crap I can do with your mind. I could make you see them, just like I can make you see me. You were certainly eyeing me in that French lace nightgown last night. It was fun leading you on. By the way, you looked hilarious, humping the bed like a horny bunny when there was no one there under you."

I ignored her jibe and plowed on with my questions. "Your cousins?"

"Oh, they were real enough, until you made them dead too. I'm surprised they are not here helping me torment you. But Randy and his wife were cretins. We were never really close."

"And Marilyn Zephyr?"

"My friend Marilyn is really dead, thanks to you. I merely confused you as to which house you were running into. And maybe I made her look a little like me in your eyes. She looked good as a redhead, don't you think?"

I gave her a cold stare. "Then you're the one responsible for Marilyn's death, not me."

"*Tsk, tsk.* You're the one who pulled the trigger, dear boy."

"What about you and Fred Woolworth? I knew you were a slut when I married you, but I didn't expect you to screw my partner."

"It was the other way around. He screwed me, now he's trying to screw you. Funny, isn't it."

CHAPTER 35

Did I forget to tell you this was a ghost story? No matter, this is still what happened.

I exorcized my wife.

No, I didn't sprinkle her with Holy Water or call in a priest. Being she wasn't Catholic, I figured those thing might not work on her anyway.

The solution turned out to be easier than I expected: Simply ask her to leave.

I found this in a book appropriately called *How to Rid Your House of Ghosts and Spirits*. I found it in Klett's New Age and Occult Section. It stated:

"The easiest and generally the most effective way of getting a ghost to leave your home or place of business, once you know what type of ghost with which you're dealing, is simply to talk to it. Sounds too simple, I know; however, it works in many cases …

"Sit down and gently explain to the ghost that they are deceased and that there is no reason for them to be there. Tell them that they belong on the Other Side, and encourage them to go into the light. Keep in mind that you may have to repeat this several times before the spirit chooses to leave."

So that's what I did.

"Dear, you've had your fun. Now you've gotta leave," I said in my most reasonable voice.

She was sitting on the sofa, listening to me with a concerned expression on her face. "But I was having such a good time watching you try to kill me over and over with no results. I wish I'd had that talent the first time around, when the bomb got me."

"Sorry about that, but I was very upset about your and Fred's affair. You can understand that, can't you?"

She cocked her head. "Don't you think a bomb was a bit of an overreaction? That fling meant nothing."

"Well, you know I've always been impulsive."

"A drama queen, you mean. But I suppose you wouldn't have been so upset if you hadn't loved me."

"True."

"Then why did you keep trying to kill me after you'd already succeeded?"

"I didn't know the bomb had killed you. And completing the task became somewhat obsessive. I blame the lobotomy. It screwed up my thinking."

"As I told you, the de-braining was all Freddie's doing."

"I see that now. After you go away, I will deal with him. Before long you may bump into him on the Other Side."

"Ugh. You're not making my going back sound very appealing. It was already over between me and that egotistical jerk."

"Have a nice journey."

"Bye," she said.

Then, before my eyes she began to fade. I could see through her like a movie image projected against the wall. Going, going, gone.

"See you around," I said. But there was no one there to hear me.

"Death" said Hamlet, is "that undiscovered country from whose bourne no traveler returns." How wrong he was.

CHAPTER 36

Frederick Woolworth looked surprised when I strode into the office with a cheery *hi*!

"I thought you were going to take some time off," he said, confusion showing on his narrow face.

"Didn't want to leave you in the lurch. I thought I would help Randy – I mean Sandy – catch up on the Easy Bake Oven, then kick back for a while like you suggested."

"Oh, okay."

Martha (the former Mitzi) held up her hand to flash a big diamond. "John, did you see my engagement ring?"

"Nice," I said, wondering where Sandy got enough money for a rock like that. Obviously, he had been working with my partner to rob me blind. I would have had an auditor come in to check the books if I'd thought the company would be around that long.

Woolworth walked me back to the Project Room. At the entrance I paused to study the construction. The walls were thin, just sheetrock that had been thrown up to section off the workspace. Good, I told myself.

"Keep an eye on Randy," said Woolworth. "He's not as meticulous in his work as you were."

"I thought his name was Sandy," I said.

"No, what makes you think that?"

There he was, gaslighting me again. Guess he was counting on the lobotomy to keep me confused. I had to admit, it was doing a pretty good job.

"And the girl out front is –?"

"Mitzi. I thought you knew that."

"Got a question ...."

"Shoot," he invited me to proceed with it.

"Did I actually have a lobotomy?"

He shrugged, making up his mind how much to tell me. "After the concussion from the bomb blast, the doctors elected to do a partial lobotomy. They didn't go deep. They barely touched your prefrontal cortex."

"What was the purpose?"

"Oh, medical reasons. You were in a coma. It may have been to relieve pressure on the brain. Or to help you avoid remorse over the fact you killed your wife. I'm not sure. But the doctors recommended it, so I signed the papers. Your Living Will gave me the authority to make such decisions in your behalf."

"I didn't have a Living Will."

"So I fudged a little."

"Fred, I'm aware you're trying to get me declared incompetent so you can take over the company. I'd imagine a lobotomy should do the trick."

"Think what you will. But you're certainly not capable of running Wonder Works in your present condition."

"My job is to invent things. I can still do that. Didn't I just come up with that Easy Bake Oven using molecular friction?"

"Hate to burst your bubble, but Sandy came up with that. We were just letting you think you had contributed something to keep you calm and out of the way."

"I thought you just said his name was Randy."

"Randy, Sandy. His real name is Carl – Carl Gibson. I hired him away from Ideas Unlimited to replace you."

"What was wrong with me? Before the lobotomy, I mean."

Frederick Woolworth rolled his eyes. "You name it. I had a buyer for the company, but you didn't like the offer. You were selfish and greedy. The company didn't need you or your negative attitude once I had Carl in place."

"Is he really engaged to Mitzi – or is that more of your brain games?"

"Carl is gay as a goose. And Darlene – that's her real name – is *my* girlfriend."

"I thought my wife was your girlfriend."

"Oh, you know about that too? We had a fling, mostly a way for me to get inside information about you. But I had dropped her by the time you blew her to Kingdom Come. You actually did me a favor with that. She could have become a problem. She was very clingy."

"Tell me about it. I've had a helluva time getting rid of her."

"So where do we go from here? You may as well sign over the company or I will proceed with a competency hearing. In the end, you'll be out on your butt. And possibly in a loony bin."

"Let me think about it. This is a lot to take in. And my ol' noggin' ain't the well-oiled machine it used to be."

"Sure, but I want to know where we stand by end of day. Otherwise, I will call my lawyer first thing in the morning. He already has all the papers drawn up, ready for my signature."

"Mind if I hang out with Carl while I mull this over. I'd like to see how he solves a few kinks with the oven. Quantum physics can be counter intuitive. You touch something over here, it moves something over there. Results are hard to predict."

"Go have fun. Exercise your brain. What little you have of it left."

"You don't have to belittle me. I was once a pretty good inventor, judging by all those citations and awards on my office wall."

"Not anymore. Those days are gone, old bean. Like I say, go have fun with Carl. I'll check back around five."

I watched as the smug bastard walked away, heading up front, probably to flirt with his girlfriend. Guess I had finally figured out what Mitzi A/K/A Darlene really did.

~ ~ ~

"Hi Carl," I said as I stepped into the Project Room.

"My name's Randy," he corrected me. Maybe he was a Method Actor, always staying in character.

"Whatever. Mind if I watch you work?"

"Just stay out of the way. I'm at a delicate stage."

"You mean it could blow up?"

"Not likely. No explosion here with this oven."

I sidled over to the table in the corner. "How about here?" I said, pushing the red detonation button.

"Wait!" Carl/Randy/Sandy screamed. "What the heck are you doing?"

A glowing **3** appeared on a tiny LED screen, then a **2**, then a **1**, then ...

... the bomb went off!

~ ~ ~

The experts say, "An explosion is an extremely rapid release of energy accompanied by a shock wave. This shock wave consists of highly compressed air traveling radially outward from the source at supersonic velocities. As the wave expands, pressures decrease rapidly (with the cube of the distance) and when it meets a surface in line-of-sight of the explosion, it is amplified by a factor of up to thirteen."

The bomb had been made for testing the Explosive Ordnance Disposal blast suit. It contained two pounds of fine aluminum powder mixed with ammonium nitrate to produce a 50-pound bomb capable of mass casualties and destruction in the room in which it is exploded.

Last time, even wearing the EOD suit, I had received a serious concussion and my wife who was unprotected got literally blown to pieces. This had been the same size bomb as that.

The explosion practically took the building down, knocking apart the thin sheetrock walls, blowing out the double-pane front windows, and toppling over my Dodge Charger which was parked in the owner's space out front.

Of course, everybody died.

CHAPTER 37

Yes, I'm dead. I told you this was a ghost story.

So is ol' Fred, as well as Randy and Mitzi (or whoever the hell they were).

I like it on the Other Side. My thinking is no longer confused. I guess I got the death sentence that I deserved, justice served.

I haven't seen my wife yet, nor any of the others I'd killed. But apparently I haven't completed my journey to the final destination. I'm still here, where I can screw with *your* mind, make you see me as if I'm real, do all kind of crazy things.

I suppose I will move on soon enough, but I'm here for now ...

... haunting you, dear reader.

Author's Afterword

I hope you enjoyed this lighthearted attempt at a ghost story. Its origins are easily traceable to that popular movie *The Sixth Sense*. That's the one where the protagonist doesn't know he's dead until the very end. I wanted to try a reversal of that theme, where the protagonist doesn't know that his wife is really dead – with a little joke on the reader added at the very end.

This required a variation on that literary device known as the Unreliable Narrator. An unreliable narrator is a narrator whose credibility is compromised.

There are several kinds, this one being closest to a subset called The Madman. As *The International Journal of Social Science and Humanities Research* describes it, this is "a narrator who is either only experiencing mental defense mechanism, such as (post-traumatic) dissociation and self-alienation, or severe mental illness such as schizophrenia or paranoia." Examples include *Das Cabinet des Dr. Caligari*, Franz Kafka's self-alienating narrators, Edgar Allan Poe's *The Tell-Tale Heart*, and noir fiction's cynical detective who unreliably describes his own emotions.

In this case, John (our protagonist) sometimes misspeaks due to his medical condition, but his wife cannot be believed at all as she switches her story with non-stop regularity.

The other reference, of course, is to the movie *Gaslight*. Gaslighting can be described as the subjective experience of having one's reality repeatedly questioned by another. John experiences that, thanks to both his wife and his devious business partner.

If you guessed what was going on early in the story, good for you. I assume you plowed on to see if you were right. We writers use all kind of tricks to get you to stick with us from Page 1 to the end of the book.

I was taught in school that reading should be fun. I guess I still believe that. So, while this little trifle won't win the Booker Award or even be mentioned in the pulpy pages of *Fangoria* Magazine, I hope you had fun reading it. That's what I was aiming for.

As they say to contestants on a game show, "Thank you for playing along."

-H.L. Osterman

Thank you for reading.
Please review this book. Reviews
help others find Absolutely Amazing eBooks and
inspire us to keep providing these marvelous tales.
If you would like to be put on our email list
to receive updates on new releases,
contests, and promotions, please go to
AbsolutelyAmazingEbooks.com and sign up.

ABOUT THE AUTHOR

Howard Lowell Osterman collected a few rejection slips from popular magazines before deciding he preferred the steady salary of a staff writing position with a newspaper. That led to other "writing gigs" with magazines and book publishers. "A good living," Osterman tells it. "But in my spare time I kept cranking out sensational novels and short stories. My dirty little secret, I call them, usually working under pseudonyms to avoid conflicts with employers looking for a pound of flesh." He has lived in New York, Chicago, and Daytona. He enjoys watching old *film noir* movies. He hopes one day to write a screenplay.

For sales, editorial information, subsidiary rights information
or a catalog, please write or phone or e-mail

AbsolutelyAmazingEbooks
Manhanset House
Shelter Island Hts., New York 11965, US
Tel: 212-427-7139
www.BrickTowerPress.com
bricktower@aol.com
www.IngramContent.com

For sales in the UK and Europe please contact our distributor,
Gazelle Book Services
White Cross Mills
Lancaster, LA1 4XS, UK
Tel: (01524) 68765 Fax: (01524) 63232
email: jacky@gazellebooks.co.uk

www.ingramcontent.com/pod-product-compliance
Lightning Source LLC
Chambersburg PA
CBHW051511260626
47162CB00008B/2918